THE AMISH SCHOOL TEACHER

AMISH WOMEN OF PLEASANT VALLEY BOOK 6

SAMANTHA PRICE

AMISH ROMANCE

Bishop Elmer Shroder and his wife Hannah have thirteen children.
Timothy is their eldest son, who is now married to Abigail. Abigail was a widow who already had a young daughter, Ferris.

May is about to marry Jeff Whiley, and her twin, April, is married to Phillip and soon expecting their first child. Simon and Sandra are May and April's long-suffering parents.

Rebecca, the bishop's second child and only daughter, is the community's midwife, married to Jacob, and step-mother to Micah. Jacob's sister, Anne, lives with them and minds Micah while Rebecca works.

Samuel Kauffman and Mary are married and their secret

about Lois being Mary's real child is out. Together Samuel and Mary now have baby, Sam.

William Bronstein is a widower with two children, Ivy and Grace. His two sisters are Elizabeth and Nancy.

Karen is married to Jason Shroder, the bishop's nephew, and they are expecting their second set of twins.

CHAPTER 1

DURING THE SUNDAY MEETING, William Bronstein sat one row in front of Deborah Morris. He, of course, was on the men's side of the Yoders' living room. Deborah tried to stop her eyes from wandering toward him because she didn't want anyone to notice she was looking. The last thing she wanted was for somebody to discover her love for William especially when she taught his two girls. Not only would that be embarrassing, it might also upset the school board. The school board was a group made up of church oversight and older community members. Deborah had been the schoolteacher for over ten years and took the role seriously.

At thirty-three, she was unmarried and, with most girls in the community being married before the age of twenty, she was an anomaly. She knew it was her plain appearance and shyness with men that held her back. With mousy brown hair, a somewhat sallow complexion, and non-descript gray eyes, she knew she was no beauty. And the chances of finding a husband lessened with every passing day.

Still, she had hopes that the widower, William Bronstein, would notice her one day. Sure, they talked, but only as teacher to parent and she was working on that escalating to friendship. After becoming friends, he might fall in love with her.

Deborah remembered William's late wife quite well. She could scarcely think of William without the image of the pretty woman whose spirals of golden hair always escaped from the confines of the *kapp* framing her perfect oval face. Nita's skin had been flawless and her eyes the bluest of blues. With that image, one that Deborah could not shake, it was hard to continue her hopes of one day becoming his wife. Praying was what she did to keep her flame of hope ignited.

William's daughters had to be a constant reminder to him of his dear wife especially since they looked so much like their mother.

"What's wrong?" May whispered.

She smiled at May, realizing she'd been looking in William's direction for far too long. "Nothing at all. I'm just a little tired." Her head turned to the front of the room where Bishop Elmer was delivering the word. He disliked it when people whispered instead of listening and he often stopped talking and waited until those whispering amongst themselves stopped. Of course, that was most embarrassing for the people involved and she didn't want that happening to her since she had a certain reputation to uphold. Being the schoolteacher, people expected her to behave in a certain manner. Perfectly. Even though she fixed her eyes on Bishop Elmer, out of the corner of her eye she still managed to watch William.

As usual, at the Amish church meetings held in the members' homes, men sat on one side and the women on the other. Even the children were separated boys from girls. Sons would sit with their fathers, daughters with their mothers. Sometimes children sat with other relatives or close family friends. Today, William's daughters sat with his sisters, Elizabeth and Nancy, in the very front row. Elizabeth was visiting from Walnut Creek now that her husband was better and nearing the end of his recovery from a sudden stroke. It was because of Elizabeth's visit that Deborah hadn't seen William in days. Elizabeth had taken on the task of collecting the children from school.

When the meeting was over, May and Deborah slid along to the end of the bench while Abigail, who had been sitting on the other side of May was busy talking to someone else. May touched Deborah's arm lightly. "Are you sure you're all right?"

"*Jah.* Why do you keep asking?"

"You seem a little distracted and not yourself."

Deborah smiled at her young friend. They'd become close since May had started helping at the school. Now, Deborah didn't know how long May would continue in that role since she was marrying Jeff in a week and a half. "I'm fine. You should stop thinking about me and start concentrating on your wedding."

3

May giggled. "I'm excited. And April is coming back—there's enough time before she has the *boppli*, did I tell you that?"

"Only about fifty times last week, and this makes fifty-one."

As they walked out of the house laughing together, May said, "I wonder what it's like to be pregnant. I mean, be carrying a child, not the birth part." She shrugged. "Having something growing inside you must feel very strange."

That was something Deborah hoped to learn firsthand one day. "What does April say about it?"

"Not much. She said, in her letters I mean, it's a bit strange. When she gets back here, she'll be so much bigger. It'll be strange to see her like that. She was always so skinny."

"I guess so." While May had been talking, Deborah's eyes had wandered again to William. He was talking to his sisters as he walked out of the house, and his girls were with them. She pulled her attention away from William to share in the excitement of May's upcoming wedding. "Are the wedding dresses finished yet?"

"*Jah*, they were finished on Friday. The last stitch was sewn. I told you that on Friday."

"Oh, I'm sorry, May. I suppose I am distracted lately."

"What's going on? I'm sure something is. You can tell me."

"It's nothing much."

May raised her eyebrows. "I'm not so sure about that. Anyway, I've decided to have dinner on Wednesday night for all my friends. Will you be able to make it?"

"What is it?"

"It's a kind of pre-wedding dinner. Only girls are invited."

Deborah smiled. "That sounds like fun. When did you decide this?"

"Just then." May giggled. "I've been thinking about whether to have one or not and just then I decided it'd be a good idea. I think you need cheering up."

"Ah, you're doing this for me?"

"For both of us. It's my wedding and I'll only get married once, so I can do anything I like."

"I suppose you're right."

They walked to the food table together. There was always a meal served after the Sunday meetings. As Deborah took a plate to help herself, William's girls ran up to her.

"Hello, Miss Deborah."

"Hello, girls. How are you enjoying your aunt's visit?"

"Very much. *Dat* even lets us stay up longer at night," Grace said.

"*Jah*, an extra half hour," Ivy added.

"Really?"

They both nodded enthusiastically.

Then Ivy frowned. "I don't know why I have to go to sleep at the same time as Grace. I'm older, so I should be able to stay up later."

"Don't you both share a room?"

The girls nodded.

"It makes sense you go to bed at the same time if you're sharing the same room, don't you think?"

Ivy's eyes opened wide. "Do you mean if I had my own room I would be able to stay up later?"

Deborah giggled, realizing she was digging herself a hole, and William might not be too happy with her. "I don't know, Ivy. That would be up to your *vadder*."

Ivy didn't even say goodbye as she raced away followed closely by Grace. Deborah glanced over and saw them heading to their father.

May had heard the whole thing and laughed. "See what you've done?"

Deborah giggled. "Oh *nee*. I hope they don't tell him I suggested it."

"Well, you didn't really suggest it."

"I know, but that's how it'll sound."

"Deborah, this is something I haven't asked you, but …"

Deborah frowned at her. "This seems serious. Are you leaving me and *die schul?*" It had taken Deborah and the school board a long time to find someone who wanted to help out for a few hours a week, and May was good at what she did. Deborah didn't want to lose her.

May shook her head. *"Nee,* that's just it. I was going to ask you if I could stay on."

Deborah put her hand to her head. "Of course I want you to stay. You gave me a fright. I thought you were going to say you wanted to leave."

"Nee. I never want to leave. I'm enjoying the children so much. Maybe one day there'll be so many children in the community that they'll need two teachers."

Deborah nodded, trying to be encouraging, but she knew it would be a long time before that happened.

"Maybe. I hope so. Although, the board seems set on unmarried women as the teachers. I'm glad they haven't said anything about you still helping me after your wedding."

"Who are you going to sit with?" May asked Deborah.

Deborah knew May wanted to sit with Jeff. "You go, I'll find someone to sit with."

"Are you sure?"

"Of course."

Just as she sat down, William walked over to her and sat down in front of her. She looked up at him wondering why he was by himself and had no food. He spoke first. "Ivy tells me you suggested she have her own room."

Deborah put a hand over her mouth and giggled. "I'm sorry. I didn't handle that one very well."

He shook his head and by his deadpan expression she could see he wasn't happy. She told him what she said to his daughter, and then added, "She's a bright girl and came up with the idea that in separate rooms she might be allowed to stay up later. I didn't actually suggest it. Do you see?"

Now his face softened. "I do see. That's not quite the way I heard it."

Deborah shrugged her shoulders.

"I'm sorry. I hope you don't think I was accusing you of anything. You see, I like to have our spare room kept as a guest room. And then there is her sewing room that I like to keep just how she left it."

Deborah didn't need to hear about 'her' at this point. It seemed odd he didn't say Nita's name as though the act of doing so would bring him sorrow. "There's no need to explain." Now she could see how much William was still in love with his late wife. The situation seemed hopeless if he wanted to keep his house just how it used to be. How could she compete with William's late wife if she was still alive in his heart?

CHAPTER 2

DEBORAH HAD TRIED to get to May's place early for dinner, but her horse had thrown a shoe and she'd had to use her spare who was in the top paddock. Today she'd be late, which was something she never liked to do. Being a schoolteacher had taught her to be punctual.

She made her way to May's with a gift for her. It was a white linen tablecloth that she had kept in her hope chest for quite some years. *Almost twenty years,* Deborah figured. *Somebody might as well get some use out of it.*

The two women embraced and then Deborah handed her the gift. May's face lit up as she took it from her. "You shouldn't have done this. I didn't even think to say no gifts."

Deborah looked around and saw that nobody else had brought presents. "It doesn't matter; it's nothing big just a little something I had lying around the *haus.*"

"*Denke.*" She opened it and marveled at the fine sewing

on the hem of the tablecloth. "Are you sure you don't want to keep it?"

"*Nee.* I was going to give it to you soon, anyway."

"It's so lovely."

"Come on, May," a girl called out.

May looked over her shoulder and then looked back at Deborah. "Come along." She took Deborah's arm and headed toward the kitchen. "There are food and cake in here; help yourself and then come and join us in the living room."

Deborah put her hand to her head. "I didn't even think to bring a plate."

"That was not necessary. *Mamm* and I cooked everything except for the cakes. We bought them from the markets."

While Deborah was busy helping herself to food, May walked back into the living room. Deborah was left in the kitchen with May's mother and the bishop's aunt, who had become "Aunt Agatha" to the whole community.

They stopped talking to one another, and then Aunt Agatha asked her, "How's May doing with her school duties?"

"She is doing wonderfully well. So well that she's gone from volunteering to being paid for several hours per week."

"That's very good." Aunt Agatha smiled and nodded to May's mother.

"She's loving it too," May's mother, Sandra, said. "She's always talking about the children and what they're learning."

"She comes in early nearly every day. She's such a help."

Aunt Agatha said, "Once she gets married, she won't be able to be there as much."

Sandra smiled. "I'm sure she will; she loves it."

"Jah, she does but then the *bopplis* will start coming along."

That comment caused Sandra to gasp with delight. "Oh, I can't wait for the little ones. And with April living so far away I've been so upset, but now May's getting married and I'll have some of my *grosskinner* living close."

Deborah laughed. "I'm sure there will be many *kinner,* between the two of them. Maybe even some twins."

Sandra gasped. "Oh, *jah,* twins."

"And what about you?" Aunt Agatha took a step toward Deborah, who looked up from placing a sausage on her plate.

"What about me?"

"Marriage and *kinner?"*

"I'll be at the school forever. That has passed me by. I'm too old."

"That's not true," Aunt Agatha said.

May's mother excused herself and left the kitchen when she heard squeals coming from the other room.

Deborah was hoping Aunt Agatha would also go to see what the commotion was all about, but she didn't budge and her eyes were still fixed beadily on Deborah. There was nothing else for Deborah to do but finish the conversation. "At this point, I'll be at *die schul* forever. No one has wanted to marry me so far." She shrugged her shoulders and told the truth. "I'm not happy about it, but that's just the way things are."

Aunt Agatha shook her head. "I'm sure there have been lots of men who've wanted to marry you. You're just fussy, that's all."

Deborah smiled and put a little more food on her plate, pleased that some people might have though she was single because she was fussy. The truth was she had never even been asked on a buggy ride, not even once.

"No one is courting you at this time?" Aunt Agatha asked.

Deborah gave an exasperated sigh.

Aunt Agatha raised her eyebrows. "Forgive me if I'm being too nosy."

"It's all right, you're not. I can tell you that I'm not dating anybody and I'm not even close to it. I fear that time and chances have passed me by and that's all there is to it."

"Nonsense!" Agatha pressed her lips tightly together. "There are many men suited to you in this very community."

Deborah thought hard and couldn't even think of one, besides William. "I don't think so."

Aunt Agatha rattled off a few names. One was a single man, Mervin Breuer, who lived with his grandmother and rarely left his home. No one knew if he was shy, or whether he was just not looking for a wife. The other three were older, much older, and Agatha didn't even mention William's name. If Aunt Agatha didn't see them together, maybe she should let go of that hope in her heart. Not wanting to reveal her crush on William, she said, "I don't think any of them are suitable."

When May squealed again, Aunt Agatha shook her head in disapproval. "I wish she would stop those high-pitched noises. She'll have to now she's getting married; she's not a child anymore."

"I'm sure she's just excited about something." Deborah turned to leave the room. "I'll see what it's all about."

Before she took a step, Agatha mumbled, "Then again, there's always William Bronstein."

Not knowing what to say, Deborah turned back and gave a smile, and then rearranged some of the food on her plate. Agatha wasn't stupid, she knew Deborah liked him— or thought Deborah should like him. "I suppose so. I'll go see what the squeals are about. They're telling stories I'm sure. Are you coming or staying in the kitchen?"

"You can't fool me, Deborah Morris."

"What do you mean?"

"I saw that flicker of your eyes when I said William Bronstein's name. Many a time I've also seen you staring longingly in his direction."

Deborah averted her gaze. "It's true. I am fond of him. I didn't mean to lie just now. It's just that I didn't want anybody to know."

A look of delight spread over Aunt Agatha's face. "Your secret's safe with me, don't worry." She stepped a little closer to Deborah. "And does he like you too, do you think?"

CHAPTER 3

DEBORAH SHOOK HER HEAD. "I know that he doesn't. We talk to one another when he collects the girls from school, but that's the sum of it. I know he's even asked a woman for dinner with him and the girls, but he's never, ever, asked me—not even as his daughters' teacher. Not only is he not interested, he has a distinct lack of interest in me. And I don't think there's anything I can do about it."

"The problem is he sees you, but he doesn't *see* you. He doesn't see the kind-hearted and loving woman you are."

"*Denke,* Aunt Agatha. That's kind of you to say that."

Aunt Agatha raised her hand. "I'm not finished yet. And that's because he only sees his daughters' teacher."

Her words struck Deborah's heart. Could that be true? She put her food down on the table. She was sure she could trust Aunt Agatha to keep things to herself. She was Bishop Elmer's aunt after all. "Between you and me, I know William asked May to dinner at his place before she became involved with Jeff. I think he liked May, and she was teaching at the school by that time, so I don't know if what you're saying is right."

Aunt Agatha whispered, "I sincerely doubt he would've been interested in a young girl like May. And if he was, he didn't see May as a teacher, just a temporary teacher. He sees you as *the* teacher."

"I would like to believe you, but I don't want or need any more false hope." She turned around to make sure nobody was coming into the kitchen. "I do like him and I'd be so embarrassed if anybody found out."

"Your secret's safe with me, Deborah Morris."

Deborah inhaled deeply. "Good. I thank you for that."

"Now, what are we going to do about it?"

Deborah picked up her plate of food. "There's nothing to do about it. I can't make someone like me."

"You can't, that's true, but you can open his eyes."

She was grateful for Aunt Agatha trying to help, but he'd made no move for three years. The situation was as good as hopeless. "What if his eyes are open and he doesn't like what he sees?"

"Nonsense." Aunt Agatha shook her head emphatically. "Just leave it to me."

Deborah gasped. "You're not going to tell him, are you?"

"*Nee,* of course I won't. I'll have the both of you over for dinner next week."

Deborah smiled. A dinner with him would be good. It would be a chance to spend more time with him. "Okay, *denke.*"

"And I want you to look as pretty as you can."

There it was again, the heart of the problem. The real

issue was her looks, and even Aunt Agatha knew it. "I don't have much to work with."

"Perhaps …" Aunt Agatha looked her up and down. "Perhaps a new dress?"

Deborah had been saving money to upgrade her buggy and she hadn't spent money on her clothing in quite some time. She nodded, recalling the material she'd bought two years ago intending to make a dress, but had never gotten around to it. Now might be just the time. "I could make a new dress by then."

"I notice you always wear green, and it doesn't do anything to flatter your coloring."

Deborah looked down at her dark green dress. She found it practical to have all her dresses the same color, almost like having a set of uniforms to wear. It had never entered her mind to wear a different color. The fabric she had at home was the same color and that meant she'd have to use part of her new buggy money to buy some new fabric. If it caused William to look twice at her, it would be a good investment. "What color do you suggest?"

"Blue. It would make your eyes light up."

Deborah gasped. "Blue! Married women and brides wear blue. I couldn't."

"Couldn't you? Maybe that's just the jolt he needs."

Deborah covered her mouth and giggled. "I just couldn't. Not with May getting married, and of course her dress is going to be blue."

Aunt Agatha drew her eyebrows together, deepening the furrows on her brow. "No one owns blue."

Deborah laughed at how ridiculous the whole thing

sounded. Although, she intended to go along with Agatha's suggestion, as long as she didn't have to wear blue. "Is there another color that you can suggest?" Aunt Agatha studied her for a moment while Deborah's attention was drawn to the squeals continuing in the next room. "I wonder what …?"

"Whatever it is, it's not nearly as important as what you and I are talking about. Now, let's see. Green does nothing for you, so what is the opposite to green?"

"I'm not sure." Deborah thought back to the color wheel she used at school when the younger children were learning about colors. "Red is opposite to green."

Aunt Agatha held her heart. "Oh my! Elmer would surely have a heart attack if any person in the community wore red. It's far too bold."

Deborah laughed at Agatha's reaction. "You did ask what was the opposite to green."

"Grape! It's like red, but it's the color of fruit and therefore it's acceptable."

Deborah wondered why red wasn't worn by Amish women when it was the color of apples and strawberries. Apparently, the answer was simple; it drew too much attention. "I never thought of wearing grape before."

Aunt Agatha peered into her face. "It would suit you much better. And perhaps, don't make it so roomy." She pulled out the sides of Deborah's dress.

"My clothes are only like this because I lost a lot of weight."

"That was a long time ago. Don't you have any new dresses?"

"There's not much point in making anything new when the old dresses are still good."

Aunt Agatha's eyes sparkled. "More girls should be like you."

It felt good to have Agatha's approval. "I guess I could've taken them in a little at the sides."

"You could've, but you're a sensible and practical girl and a man with any sense would appreciate that."

"I'll get the material tomorrow after *schul* and I'll start sewing a new dress right away."

"Very good, and I'll ask him for dinner on Tuesday night."

"Are you going to tell him I'm coming for dinner as well?"

Aunt Agatha tilted her head and thought about it for a while before she spoke. *"Nee,* I won't. I just want him to see you there unexpectedly and then his mind will be off you being a teacher."

"Okay. I hope it works."

"His girls like you, don't they?"

"All of my students like me. Sometimes they get into trouble, but I'm a fair teacher and they know the boundaries and they respect me."

"Good answer."

Deborah smiled once again at the older lady's approval.

"Let's go and see what all this squealing's about, shall we?"

"Jah, let's." Deborah popped a morsel of food into her mouth, feeling much more hopeful about William than she'd been for years. The screaming, they soon found out,

was due to May dashing about while two of her young friends tried to force her to eat celery. When Aunt Agatha joined in with May's mother to tell the girls to keep the noise down, the girls insisted May should eat some celery because it would keep blemishes away for the wedding day.

"Let them go," Deborah said to May's mother. "They're having a good time. Why don't we go back to the kitchen and leave them to it?"

"Jah, that would be a good idea," said Aunt Agatha.

Deborah joined the two older ladies as they sat down in the kitchen with the door closed, blocking out the noise. Sometime later, everyone migrated into the kitchen. It wasn't long before their attention turned to Deborah as each one suggested which bachelor or widower she should marry.

CHAPTER 4

IN TWO EVENINGS Deborah had managed to complete her new grape-colored dress.

Deborah tried on her newly sewn dress once again. It had been some time since she'd worn a dress that fitted properly. This was the first one she'd made for herself since she'd lost weight. Being at school every day had changed her eating habits, she realized when she wondered why she was slimmer than before.

Nervousness bubbled excitedly within her. Soon, she'd be sitting at Aunt Agatha's dining table looking directly into William's handsome face. He was a tall man, strongly built with broad shoulders just the kind of looks Deborah admired.

After taking a deep breath, she reached behind her back and did up the neckline fastenings. Her other dresses ended just a few inches above her ankles and she had wanted this one to be different, so she'd made it a couple of inches shorter just to give it a different look. Even though no one would notice, it made her feel more of a woman rather than a schoolteacher. Perhaps if she saw herself differently, so too would William.

She smoothed her dress down, enjoying the feel of the cool soft material. Then she brushed out her freshly washed and dried hair, divided it into two, and then tightly braided each half. Once she had two thigh-length plaits, she wound them and pinned them close to her head, to fit under her prayer *kapp.*

When she'd tied her *kapp* strings into a bow, she pulled on her black stockings and then slipped her feet into the lace-up shoes that she had polished twice for the occasion.

"There. All done." She leaned against the bedroom wall and prayed that if William was the right man everything would go perfectly tonight.

Deborah pulled open her front door and jumped with fright as she came face-to-face with a familiar man. She stepped back in shock with her hand over her heart. "Andrew Byler!" Moving forward, she wrapped her arms around him and hugged him, and then she stepped back, embarrassed. "Oh, I'm sorry."

He chuckled. "Don't be. That's the kind of hellos I like."

"You gave me quite a start. I surely didn't expect to see you. Why are you here? Have you come back to stay?"

"I'm moving back here. Well, have moved back here. That's the plan."

"Really?"

"*Jah.* I never said I was going forever."

"I know, but you've been gone for such a long time. What is it? Fourteen years?"

"Correct. Fourteen years and two months and three days."

"Keeping count were you?"

He nodded. "Keeping track of the days until I could come back to see you."

Deborah giggled. He had always been a joker.

He looked her up and down. "You look good. Going somewhere?"

"I'm going to Aunt Agatha's."

His face lit up. "She's a marvelous cook. She's having people over for dinner, is she?"

The last thing she wanted was for anyone else to join them. *"Nee,* just me. As far as I know." So desperate was she to have William's full attention tonight that she did something of which she did not approve—told a lie. And, it wasn't a white lie to save hurting somebody's feelings, it was a selfish lie. More of a gray lie, and it slipped right out of her mouth as though she was well practiced in the art of fibbing. "She wanted to have a talk with me about something." She shrugged her shoulders. "I've got no idea what it's about."

"I won't intrude. I like to stay out of women's stuff." He glanced down at her dress. "You look lovely. You've lost weight."

She couldn't stop the giggle that escaped her lips. She was not used to getting compliments about her appearance. *"Denke,* and *jah,* I have. I didn't try to lose weight, it just happened. What brings you back here?"

"It'll take too long to tell you if you're heading out."

"I wish we could stay and talk but I need to get to Agatha's house."

He looked back at her horse and buggy. "Don't let me stop you. You've still got Jasper I see?"

"He's semi-retired but I've been using him for the last few days because my new horse, Jingles—the dark chestnut over there in the paddock–has thrown a shoe and I haven't had time to do anything about it."

"Good thing for you that I showed up. Would you like me to take him to the blacksmith for you tomorrow?"

"Oh, that would be so good if you could do that."

"Good, and are you still teaching?"

"You know I'm a teacher?"

"*Mamm* keeps me informed."

"I'm still the teacher. I leave very early in the morning and get back around five."

"I'll collect him during the day, then, and bring him back when he's done."

"Thank you so much. Tell Bill I'll give him the money after *schul* one day this week." Bill was the local blacksmith who took care of most of the horses in the Amish community.

"Okay."

"It's good to see you, Andrew. Everyone's missed you."

"Well, I don't know if that's true, but it's a nice thought."

"Why don't you come for dinner tomorrow night?"

"Really?"

"*Jah*, we can catch up and you can tell me everything you've been doing for the last few years."

"Okay, I'd like that. I'll bring a pie."

She giggled at the thought of him in a kitchen rolling out pastry. "Have you taken up baking?"

"Nee, my *mudder* will make us one."

"Okay. Come any time after five. That's around the time I get home. Any time after that." The invitation made her feel better about not inviting him to Aunt Agatha's. Agatha wouldn't mind an extra guest, but tonight was different.

"I'll look forward to dinner," Andrew said.

After they said their goodbyes, Deborah got into her buggy and headed down the driveway, pleased her good friend was back. She hadn't realized just how much she'd missed Andrew.

Out of all the boys in the community when she was growing up, she had chosen Andrew as the one she'd most likely marry. Those plans fell apart when he left to work with his uncle in a small community, Sandy Creek, towards Ohio.

As she traveled to Aunt Agatha's house, her stomach churned worse and worse the closer she got. In desperation, she turned her thoughts elsewhere. An image of Andrew's face jumped into her mind and she wondered what he had thought of her.

Probably 'a plain girl turned into a plain woman,' she thought.

She'd only just pulled off the road and into Agatha's driveway when she saw William's buggy coming up behind her. Talking to Andrew had made her later than she'd planned; she had hoped to have a quiet word with Agatha before William arrived. Once she had stepped down and tied her horse to the railing, she waited for him to do the same.

He looked across at her. "I didn't know you were coming here too, Deborah."

"Well, here I am. Are you here by yourself?"

He walked toward her. "I am. You didn't mention you were coming here when I was speaking to you this afternoon."

"I didn't know you were coming, that's why." She gave a little shrug of her shoulders and hoped that would be the last lie she'd have to tell him.

Agatha appeared at the door, and called out, "You can continue that conversation inside, so I can be involved."

He looked up at her. "We're coming." Then he smiled at Deborah. "We've been told."

She nodded. "We certainly have. And we don't want to upset her." Aunt Agatha was known as a no-nonsense straightforward kind of a woman and Deborah was grateful for any help she could get from this wise woman.

Agatha led them into the living room. "You can both sit here by the fire while I finish preparing the meal." Aunt Agatha left them in uncomfortable silence, both of them on the same three-seater couch directly in front of the fire. She'd even picked up one of her cats and had carried him into the kitchen with her.

Eventually, William asked Deborah, "Is there anybody else coming, do you know?"

"I believe it's just us. She didn't mention anyone else was coming." Then to help cover up her previous lie, she added, "She didn't mention it just now when she called us in." He managed a smile, but seemed totally uninterested in anything she had to say. It was odd, since their conversation in the afternoons flowed so easily. Then it dawned on her that he realized this was a setup and he was annoyed. The moment desperately called for her to say something. "I found out May is still going to continue on at *die schul* even after she gets married."

"That's good." He nodded. "That's good. She's a fine teacher and the children get along with her so well."

"Jah, that's true. How long is your *schweschder* staying with you? Oh, and where is Elizabeth tonight?"

"Elizabeth received an invitation from Tina Miller for dinner for her and the girls, which was a coincidence." He stared at Deborah and she had to look away.

Now she was sure he was annoyed about the situation. It was obvious Tina Miller had been asked by Aunt Agatha to invite Elizabeth and the two girls for dinner. A minute later, the silence was so awful that Deborah bounded to her feet.

"I'll see if Agatha needs help in the kitchen." She hurried away before William had a chance to say anything. When she walked into the kitchen, she saw Aunt Agatha sitting at the table with three cats at her feet as she stared into space. She stood up immediately.

"Where is he?" Aunt Agatha whispered.

"There's a long silence, I'm afraid. I don't think this was a good idea. Do you need any help in here?"

"What are you doing? You should be out there getting to know him better."

Deborah knew nothing would work now. Not with the mood William was in. "It's no use."

"You go back out there now. This is your best opportunity." Aunt Agatha stared at her dress. "You took my advice."

Debra looked down at her dress. "Do you like it?"

"I do. It's very complimentary." Then Deborah was shooed away with a flick of Aunt Agatha's wrist and Deborah had no choice but to go back into the living room and sit down with William. The feeling in the room hadn't changed and Deborah was upset with herself for agreeing to the dinner.

CHAPTER 5

THE CONVERSATION DIDN'T IMPROVE at all throughout the dinner and Aunt Agatha was the one who had to do most of the talking. It wasn't long before Aunt Agatha gave up and the second half of the meal was eaten in almost complete silence. Now William was further away from her than ever. Deborah tried to console herself by acknowledging that at least she knew now that nothing would ever happen between them. There'd be no more daydreaming of being William's wife. When the long, drawn-out dinner was over, William wasted no time in leaving, making the excuse that he had to be home before his sister arrived back with the girls.

Aunt Agatha fixed a smile on her face after they had waved goodbye to William. "Well, how do you think that went?"

"Worse than dreadful." Deborah shook her head. Her first instinct was to lay blame somewhere, but no one was at fault except for herself for agreeing to the silly idea. "He didn't talk the whole time. You had to do all the talking through dinner because I exhausted myself making conversation while we were in the living room."

"I noticed you were very quiet. I thought the two of you might have had some words."

"It was nothing like that. The problem is that he's not attracted to me in the slightest."

"It's not you, Deborah, don't think that."

"If it's not me, then what is it?"

"I told you, he still sees you as a teacher."

Deborah knew that wasn't right. Tonight, he saw her as someone he was being set up with and he didn't appreciate it. If he'd been attracted to her, he surely wouldn't have minded.

"I've done everything I can. I've made this new dress specially in a different color, I've tried to be as delightful as I can, but no matter what I do he still isn't attracted to me. He seems to only want to talk to me at *schul* and that might not happen anymore now. It doesn't matter. It's just not meant to be."

"You can't give up just like that if he's the one you want."

"I can't force him to like me. You saw him just now. He did not have the attitude of a man who was interested in me." Deborah held back her tears. If Aunt Agatha hadn't been there, she would've howled in disappointment. She'd save up her tears for home.

"I'm sure things will work out."

Deborah couldn't work out what Aunt Agatha meant. "I don't see it."

Aunt Agatha closed the door, and Deborah followed

her back to the kitchen. "Maybe he's just not ready to get married to anyone."

Deborah picked up a handful of dishes and carried them to the sink. "I know that's not true because he's shown interest in other women, he's just not interested in me. And there's nothing I can do about that." She wondered when it would be polite to leave. Since William left as soon as the dessert was eaten, Deborah didn't feel as though she should leave just yet and then there were all the dishes.

"I think the two of you would be good together."

It seemed Agatha wasn't ready to give up, but Deborah certainly was. "Let's get these dishes done, shall we?" Deborah smiled, still trying not to cry as she placed the dishes on the right side of the sink.

Aunt Agatha filled the sink with water. "I can see the two of you together in my head. I have a mental picture of it and I know it can happen. What he needs is some healthy competition to win your heart."

Deborah stopped walking and turned to face Agatha. "That's just it, Aunt Agatha, no other man is interested in me. Otherwise, I would be married by now. I appreciate everything you've done to help me, I really do." She faced the table again and gathered more dishes.

"I don't think you should give up, that's all I'm saying."

"*Denke* for believing in me."

"Oh, Deborah, sometimes men can't see what's in front of their faces. They don't know what's good for them." Aunt Agatha pointed a finger at her. "But, if he were to see someone else was interested …"

31

Deborah nodded her head to the water. "The sink's full."

Agatha turned off the tap. As far as Debra was concerned, there was no point talking about men any further. At least she could satisfy herself with the fact that she had done everything possible. It would be embarrassing now to see him at school, and their after-school talks might now be a thing of the past.

"Nonsense. You won't do the dishes, Deborah. I'll just soak them and leave them till morning."

"Of course I will. I can't leave you with all this." Deborah put her hands on her hips, as she looked at all the saucepans lined up on the countertop.

"I don't mind if you want to go home now."

"*Nee*, I won't."

"You may not mind, but I do. Now, off you go. I know you're upset and don't want to hang around talking to an old lady like me. Wait a minute. You told us during dinner that Andrew's home, is that right?"

"*Jah.*" She had mentioned that briefly at the beginning of dinner for lack of anything else to talk about.

"Perfect. He's a good friend of yours?"

"He has always been a close friend and I missed him dreadfully when he left so many years ago."

"And do you have any romantic interest in him at all?"

"Not in the slightest." She stared at Aunt Agatha wondering what she was thinking.

"And is he courting anybody?"

Deborah shook her head.

"Then Andrew is the perfect man."

She frowned at Aunt Agatha. "What do you mean?"

"He's the perfect man to help you make William jealous."

Deborah screwed up her face.

Agatha stepped closer to her. "Would he do you a favor?"

"He would, but I couldn't ask him to be deceptive."

"You could just tell him you're interested in William but he doesn't pay you any mind, and you need a favor. Just seeing the two of you together could possibly spark some interest in William."

Quickly, Deborah thought it through. "But if William and I eventually do become a couple, I'll have to tell him about the deception."

"Certainly not! You and Andrew are just friends, aren't you? You can't help it if William Bronstein gets the wrong impression." She stared at Aunt Agatha and Aunt Agatha gave her a wink. "You know what I mean?" Agatha asked her.

"Oh dear. I don't think I could do something like that and I couldn't ask Andrew."

"Life is full of challenges and an interesting life is full of doing things you've never done before. It can't be easy being a teacher, and you managed to do it. And it can't have been easy for you when your parents died, but you got through it. The thing is, Deborah, I'd like nothing more than to see you happily married to the man of your choice. What do you say?"

She was pleased Agatha was taking such an interest in her life and her well being. "It's something to think about, I guess."

"Good, you do that. You think about it and see what you feel you should do."

"Whatever happens, I really appreciate tonight. It was a really kind thing for you to do for me."

"It seems *Gott* had a different plan, or a different timing, than ours tonight. The two of you didn't make a connection tonight, but only *Gott* knows what the future holds."

Deborah nodded and smiled but her secret worry was, what if God wanted her to remain single?

"Think about what I said, Deborah. And I will pray that *Gott* finds the right man for you whether it's William or somebody else."

"I do want to marry. That's the one thing I've always wanted, and that's the one thing I fear I'll never have."

"My dear girl, you must never fear anything. Where there is love there is no fear."

Deborah smiled at Aunt Agatha. It felt good to have someone on her side, helping her. "Well, I'll have to work on being less fearful."

"Do work on it, and pray on it, and I'll help you to do just that."

"Denke."

She took Deborah by the arm. "Home time for you, my girl."

Aunt Agatha led Deborah through the front doorway, down the porch steps and to the waiting buggy. Deborah leaned over and hugged Aunt Agatha. "I appreciate what you're doing for me."

"I know you're upset now, but you'll feel better once you have a good sleep."

Aunt Agatha stepped back and Deborah climbed into the buggy and took hold of the reins, and then headed down the darkened driveway lit only by the buggy lights. Throughout the long drive home, Deborah couldn't stop recalling all the awkward moments of the night. She'd never experienced so many embarrassing things in one whole day, much less in one brief night.

CHAPTER 6

THE NEXT DAY AFTER SCHOOL, it was no surprise to see William's sister, Elizabeth, collect the girls from school. In one way, it was a relief. She wouldn't have to see William again so soon—but wouldn't it just be more awkward when she finally had to face him?

Her day brightened when, just about to walk into her house, Andrew's buggy headed toward her. As much as she loved teaching, she missed having an adult to speak with during the day. And May wasn't working again until a few weeks after her wedding.

She'd forgotten she'd invited him for dinner. "You're on time?" Deborah called out.

"That's what I wanted to see you about. *Nee, Mamm* is expecting me back there for dinner. I'm so sorry. She was upset when I told her I was coming here, so I said I'd come and ask you if we could make it another night."

"Sure, that's fine by me. We can make it tomorrow. Do you have time for *kaffe?*"

"Always." He jumped down from the buggy and walked toward her. "And the report on your horse's new shoe."

"Ach, jah. I hope it went well?"

"Jah, no surprises. The other three looked good, Bill told me, and so he just did the replacement."

Over their coffee in the living room, Deborah asked, "What's the real reason you came back here?"

He chuckled. "I can't fool you, can I?"

Deborah shook her head. "I knew there was more to it."

He leaned back and put his feet up on the coffee table. "Do you mind my feet here?"

"Jah, I do mind."

"I'm sorry, I've lived by myself for far too long." He removed them, smiled and repositioned himself. "I came back because I was homesick and wanted to see my family again."

"Oh, that's rough, but I don't believe a word of it."

"I'll tell you one day. Not just yet." He stared at Deborah, and then asked, "How come you never married? I thought you would've by now. I thought I'd come back and find you married with half a dozen *kinner* running around screaming."

"First off, no *kinner* of mine would run around screaming."

He laughed. "All right, I'll leave off the screaming part, but why haven't you married?"

She looked back into his dark hazel eyes. "It's not as though I'm against the idea."

"I know what you're going to say. The right person hasn't come along, blah blah."

Deborah nodded. "Something like that." She couldn't tell him the right person had come along, but he wasn't interested.

"Maybe we should agree to marry each other if we both haven't married by forty."

"Done." She giggled. "That's my first proposal."

Andrew leaned forward. "Hopefully not your last."

She remembered what Aunt Agatha said and didn't see the harm in letting him know she liked William because he might be able to help. "Well, since we're on the subject of marriage, there is somebody I like."

"Really?"

"*Jah,* but there's no point because he pays me no mind. Someone suggested I should enlist the help of someone— someone like you—and get friendly with that someone, and see if he gets jealous." She held her breath hoping Andrew wouldn't think she was dreadful for suggesting such a thing.

"That's an old trick." He spoke in such a way that it made Deborah giggle. Then, he said, "What? You mean ... me help you make someone jealous?"

"What a good idea. It's likely brilliant. Would you do that for me?"

He laughed. "I like the way you make out like it's my idea. Is that what you were planning all along?"

"Kind of." She put her hand over her mouth and laughed.

He straightened, put his coffee mug down, and narrowed his eyes. "Who is this mystery man?"

"It's William Bronstein."

His face screwed up. "Really? I thought he was married."

"He was, but his *fraa* died a few years ago and he has two darling little girls."

"Ah, I remember now. I'd heard about that." He rubbed his forehead. "I feel dreadful for forgetting."

"They were so much older than we were. The age difference doesn't matter so much now that we're older, but back then it was a lot."

Andrew nodded. "I'll do what you want. Just tell me what you need. I put myself in your hands. You do the planning and I'll do whatever you want me to do."

This was the best result she could have hoped for. "You mean it?"

"Of course. That's what friends are for—to do awkward things for one another."

She shrugged. "I never thought of it like that, but if you say so. I'm new to this, so I'm not sure where to start."

"Hmm, we'll have to come up with a plan."

"Sounds good."

CHAPTER 7

THE NEXT DAY, Deborah drove to work in her buggy, confident and pleased to have Andrew on her side.

As usual, after school the girls waited with her for their father who was always running several minutes late. Deborah's heart beat faster when she saw William in the buggy rather than Elizabeth. She walked with the girls to his buggy. When William was out of the buggy and on the grass, the girls ran the last few steps to him. He put an arm around each girl and then looked up at Deborah, smiling. It was a pleasant if not unexpected sight to see.

"I'm sorry about that dinner the other night, William."

"It *was* rather odd." He chuckled. "I know you felt just as uncomfortable as I did."

"*Jah,* I did. I had no idea she was going to do that." Deborah pressed her lips together. "All I knew was she was having me to dinner and I didn't know who else was coming."

"Don't concern yourself. She must have got a funny idea in her head about us."

Deborah shrugged. "Possibly."

He looked down at his girls. "Did you two have a good day today?" At once, both girls started talking causing him to lift his hands. "One at a time. What have I told you?"

"Me first," Ivy said. "I'm the oldest."

"How about this? You can tell me what you did when we get into the buggy. I think I should speak to Miss Deborah. You can both sit in the buggy and wait."

The girls nodded. Most of the buggies were leaving, and a new one pulled up behind William's. Both Deborah and William looked over to see who it was.

"Is that Andrew, who used to be …?" William asked.

"Jah, it's Andrew Byler. He's back."

"What's he doing here? I haven't seen him since he left years ago."

She gave a girlish giggle. "He's here to see me."

William's eyes opened wide and he looked back at Andrew. "I see."

"Excuse me, I should speak with him. I'll see you tomorrow, girls," Deborah called out.

"Bye, Miss Deborah," the girls chorused from the back-seat of the buggy

"Bye, William." She turned and walked toward Andrew's buggy. Inside, she was glowing because of William's reaction to seeing Andrew. Was that jealousy? She climbed into Andrew's buggy.

"How did that go?" Andrew asked as he glanced over at William, who was walking to his buggy. William turned back, looked at them, and waved. Andrew lifted his hand to acknowledge him.

"He certainly seemed surprised you were back."

The corners of Andrew's lips lifted upward. *"Jah*, it seems I've surprised a lot of people. I don't know why. I never announced I was going for good."

"You've been gone for a long time."

Andrew turned to face her squarely. "Well, what are we doing? Am I driving you home?"

"Nee. I came here in my buggy. We can sit here talking until William drives off."

"I see." Andrew raised his eyebrows. "We're having a cozy conversation, are we?"

"That's right."

He chuckled. "I hope you have a better plan than this."

"I don't. This is the only one I have. We didn't come up with much last night, apart from us being seen together. Have you thought of anything else?"

"Nee."

"I'll just take things one step at a time. Why don't you tell me why you've come back now?"

His eyebrows drew together. "This is my town."

She shook her head. "I know you better than that. My guess is you had a relationship that didn't work out."

He rested his elbow on the window base of the buggy and placed his chin on his knuckles. "Well, you're half right."

"I knew it. Face me properly in case William looks back at us when he drives past."

Andrew squinted and looked at William who was turning his buggy around. "He's taking his time."

"He was probably making sure the girls were sitting quietly before he left."

"Maybe he was seeing how long we were going to be talking for."

Deborah giggled. "I hope so because that would mean our plan is working. Now, tell me about you."

"I might as well tell you what happened because I know you won't stop asking me."

"Go on."

"I was interested in a girl and we were courting for months and just when I was about to ask her to marry me —officially, I mean—she tells me she's marrying someone else." Deborah could see his eyes getting misty. "What do you think about that?" he asked.

"That's terrible. How did that come about? How did she get to know this other guy?"

"She grew up with him. He lived next to her family, and then one day he admitted how he felt about her, I guess, and then things happened from there."

"Did it come as a shock?"

"A dreadful shock. But there's nothing I can do about it."

"Did they get married?"

"Not yet. They announced they were getting married and I'll be going back at the end of the year for the wedding."

"I'm sorry."

He shook his head. "She made her choice. I only want someone who wants to be with me."

"Maybe she was confused—is confused."

"It's no use. I had to let go of the idea of being with her, entirely. I moved to get away from her, them, and everything else."

"I'm sorry things ended like that. Did you enjoy the community in Sandy Creek while you were there?"

"I did. I really liked the place. Anyway, that's my sad story. The short version of my sad story. I could tell you more, but I don't want to bore you."

Deborah smiled at him. "I thought something was wrong with you."

"A lot of things are wrong with me according to Becky."

"Becky. That's her name?"

"*Jah*, and don't mention it again. Please do me that favor?"

She nodded. "Okay I'll never mention that name again—ever."

"He's driving past us now."

"He'll drive up the road and then he'll pass us coming back because he lives behind us going that way." She pointed to the road behind her.

As William passed, Deborah pretended to be deep in conversation with Andrew. Out of the corner of her eye, she could see William staring at them.

"I think he's forgotten that dreadful dinner. It was a disaster, a complete disaster."

"I know, you told me. At least you have Aunt Agatha on your side. That must make you feel good."

Deborah pulled a face and looked behind them at William's buggy getting smaller and smaller as it moved away. "It will when something works."

"Oh, about dinner tonight. Is it okay if I make that another night?"

Deborah had forgotten again she had asked him for dinner tonight. "Sure. You've had a better offer?"

He laughed. "Not exactly. *Mamm's* asked a few family members around because she's so excited I'm back."

"Sure. We'll make it another night. Thanks for what you've done just now. I think it had the right effect on him. Time will tell."

"Anytime. Just let me know what our next move will be."

Deborah got out of Andrew's buggy and waved goodbye and then proceeded to her own horse and buggy situated around the back of the schoolhouse. She was glad Andrew had other plans for dinner because she preferred a quiet night to gather her thoughts after everything that had happened.

The way William had reacted to seeing Andrew gave her some hope. She'd known William for a long time and knew he wasn't perfect. He was self-opinionated and dogmatic, but there was something about him she'd always admired. To carry this ruse further, she would have to be seen with Andrew at the Sunday meeting, and after that, the next community event was May and Jeff's wedding.

CHAPTER 8

THE REST OF THE WEEK, Elizabeth collected the girls from school, so Deborah had no way to gauge William's thoughts.

Saturday arrived and just as Deborah was finishing loading laundry into the gas-powered washing machine at the back of the house, she heard a buggy. She flicked on the machine, and walked around the corner to see Andrew.

"Hello. I wasn't expecting you here today."

"My mother said it's meeting day tomorrow; we need to get our plan into place. I told my parents we were courting."

Deborah gasped. "You what?"

"Isn't that what you wanted?"

"I don't know." Deborah rubbed her head. She hadn't thought through all the consequences. "I mean, yes. I guess so. That's what I wanted, but I didn't think how serious this would be. Are you sure you're prepared to do this?"

"Already done. Besides, I said I would. This is what we've got to do if you really want your plan to work."

"Oh no, I just thought of something."

He stepped forward. "What is it?"

"If my plan works then everyone will think I've left you to be with William Bronstein."

"And that'll make it look like all women leave me, when the news about Becky filters through the rumor mill. Don't worry. I can deal with that."

She was more thinking of what people would think of her for being so fickle. Then she was upset with herself for being so selfish. It would look bad for Andrew as well. "Are you sure you don't mind people thinking ill of you?"

"If that happens, I'll be happy for you because you'll be with the man you love."

"This makes me feel selfish. I didn't think of how it would affect you when I asked you to do it."

"That's what friends are for, *jah?*"

"Well, some friends."

He laughed. "Why don't you make me a cup of coffee and then perhaps we should go for a drive and be seen around together? Unless you're busy today."

She smiled and nodded enthusiastically. "*Denke,* I'd like that. I was just about to do some chores, but I'll gladly leave them until later. I've just put some washing on. I'll pin it out when we get back."

As they drove away in Andrew's buggy from Deborah's

house, he said, "What I didn't tell you was that *Mamm* invited you to dinner Monday night."

"Really?" She couldn't think of anything more awkward. Yes, she could. That dinner with William the other night had to be the worst.

He nodded. "If we're going to do this we have to do it properly."

"I didn't think it through. I'm misleading your whole entire *familye*."

"There's no harm in it. We're not robbing anybody of anything." He laughed and glanced over at her. "Since when did you get so serious?"

"I've never done anything like this before. And, I'm the school teacher and I feel I must set an example of good behavior to my pupils, and everyone else."

"You've never been in love before and love does strange things to you."

"And what's your excuse? Why are you helping me?"

"My love-life didn't turn out the way I would've liked. It'll be nice to see you happy."

He truly was selfless. The years hadn't changed his kind heart. *"Denke,* Andrew. I do appreciate everything you're doing. I'm not trying to talk you out of it, believe me."

"Just be happy, Deborah. That's all I want. As far as everyone else is concerned, we're friends and now we're going to let them know we're a little more than friends. It's just a little exaggeration. No big deal."

"But now your parents think we're courting."

"They're fine, I had to tell them that. At least it'll get me out of all those *familye* dinners. Or I'll have you with me and you can be equally traumatized," he joked.

She rubbed her eyes with both hands. "I suppose you're right. I hope we're successful in this."

"We will be."

"Is your *mudder* happy about us being together at least?"

He chuckled. "She was delighted. I had to stop her making wedding plans."

Deborah covered her mouth. *"Ach nee.* This is dreadful. I hope she doesn't talk about things like that on Monday. I hope she won't be too disappointed when I leave you to be with William."

"It'll be okay. You just concentrate on William falling in love with you. Now that he's seen you with someone else, his brain might tick over."

"That's what Aunt Agatha thought. She said he needs to see me as a woman not just the person who teaches his children."

"You don't have to convince me of anything."

She laughed. "Tell me about Becky. What's she like?"

He moved the reins into one hand and stared at her. "Didn't I just ask you never to mention her name?"

"You did, but it might help you to talk about her."

He shook his head and looked back at the road. "I'm still upset about her leaving me. Every night when I went to bed I'd imagine the rest of our lives. I'd think about our *kinner* and what they'd look like. We'd talked about where we'd live and everything." He sighed.

"Did you see it coming—her leaving you?"

"Nee, I didn't. We talked a future together and she

seemed just as excited about it as I was. To this day, I don't know what went wrong and perhaps it's better I never find out."

His emotions were still obviously raw, so Deborah didn't say anything further.

After a few hours of Andrew driving Deborah around the town, six different members of their community had seen them and Andrew considered that was a day well spent. Deborah had completely forgotten about her washing, and the best drying hours of the day were already gone. She'd have to dry her laundry inside the house in front of the fire.

"I hope you're satisfied with today's efforts?" he asked, as he pulled up by her front door.

"I am. I'm grateful you're doing this for me." They both heard a buggy and turned around. It was Rebecca. "Oh, I've got a visitor. Rebecca, the bishop's daughter. Do you remember her?"

"Yeah. She was just a kid when I left."

"She's married now, with a step son, Micah. Do you want to stay for a while?"

"*Nee*. I should go and see *Mamm* and spend some time with her and *Dat*."

"Okay. Thanks again."

"You're welcome." When she got out of the buggy, he leaned over and whispered, "You must stop thanking me, and don't blow our cover. You can't tell anyone."

"I won't." She stepped back waiting for him to leave and for Rebecca's buggy to draw closer.

Andrew's buggy stayed put. "Also, we should arrive together for the meeting tomorrow."

"I never thought about that. I guess it's a good idea."

Andrew gave her a little nod, and then moved his horse forward.

The two buggies passed each other in the driveway, and when Rebecca's stopped, Deborah walked over. "Hello." She looked in the back to see if Micah was with her and he wasn't. "Where's Micah?"

"Anne's watching him. I'm on the way back from doing my rounds. I had two appointments. I've got Ruth having her baby any day now." Rebecca, the community midwife, jumped down from the buggy. "She thought she was in labor, but she wasn't. I heard you were driving around town with Andrew. Was that him just now?"

"*Jah*, it was. Andrew Byler. Do you remember him? He left when you were quite young. He hasn't been back, and we were quite good friends. He was in a hurry just now, but he'll be at the meeting tomorrow."

"Oh, it seems like you're pleased about him being back."

Deborah noticed a peculiar smile on Rebecca's face. Normally, she would've told Rebecca what was going on, but it was important no one knew. "Is that why you stopped by, you heard about us and wanted to find out—?"

"Of course not. I'm not a gossip. It's about time you found someone nice."

Deborah was pleased her plan was already working.

"Also, I always thought you would end up with somebody else."

"Who?"

Rebecca laughed. "It doesn't matter now."

"Do you have time for some iced tea?"

"Jah, I do."

"Good."

When they were in the kitchen with their iced tea, Deborah probed further. "Now, who is this person you thought I'd end up with?"

"Nee, I can't say in case you think he is totally unsuitable."

"I won't think anything bad at all."

"Okay then. It was William Bronstein."

That was exactly who Deborah hoped she would say. "Really? Why him?"

"I always thought you liked him. Well, if not always, in the last few months."

Deborah's heart sank. Was it so obvious that even Rebecca had noticed she liked him? "He's okay." Deborah couldn't admit she liked him while she was carrying out her plan with Andrew. They talked for another half hour and then Rebecca left, leaving Deborah to arrange her clean laundry in front of the fire.

CHAPTER 9

ON SUNDAY MORNING, Deborah arrived at the meeting with her new pretend boyfriend, Andrew, knowing it would cause a stir. The first thing Deborah noticed was that William's buggy was down the row from where Andrew parked his. Everyone turned and stared at them when they stepped out of the buggy.

On entering the house, they separated when Andrew moved to the men's side of the room. Then Deborah noticed May and Abigail waving to her from the back row. May and Abigail—the bishop's daughter-in-law—always sat together. Deborah sat on the other side of May after she'd greeted both girls.

"What's going on with you and that man I saw you with?" May asked.

"That's a good friend of mine. Don't you remember him?"

"*Nee.* Someone said he moved away and he's only just come back."

Deborah tried to stop the smile that was tugging at her lips. The rumors were circulating nicely.

Abigail said, "He was at Timothy's folks' *haus* the other day. I didn't get a chance to speak with him, but I saw him speaking with Bishop Elmer. Is he here to stay?"

"I'm not sure what his plans are."

May raised her eyebrows. "How come you've been keeping him a secret after I tell you everything?"

"He's no secret. We just get along well together."

May leaned closer. "Is he your boyfriend?"

"Well, he's a boy and he's a friend, so I suppose you might be able to say that he could be."

May giggled. "Why didn't you tell us at my dinner the other night instead of making us guess who you'd be suited with?"

"Everyone was having so much fun I didn't want to ruin it for everybody."

May's face beamed with delight. "This is such good news."

"It's just a friendship. Don't go thinking too far ahead. Who knows? Things might not work out between us."

Abigail leaned across, and said, "You two look perfect for one another."

"Denke." Deborah wasn't pleased about that. She didn't want to look good with anybody except William Bronstein. William was tall and handsome with broad shoulders, and Andrew, with his more boyish looks, was the opposite. "Don't get carried away. It might come to nothing."

"We won't. I don't like it either when people jump to conclusions. If you want to take it slow it's fine by me."

"Denke, May."

Then William walked into the room and Deborah didn't look at him fully because she didn't want May to guess she liked him.

"There's William and his girls," May said.

Now Deborah had no choice but to look over. "So it is, and his *schweschder* Elizabeth. She's staying with them for a while."

"She looks nothing like him."

"Well, it's his *schweschder.* Her husband's been very ill and now that he's feeling better he suggested she visit William for a week or two. She hasn't seen William for years."

"How come you know all this?" May asked.

"The girls told me before she arrived. Well, they didn't tell just me, they said it in their news time. I think it was the day after you stopped coming to *schul.*"

"In what?" Abigail asked.

They went on to explain the 'news time' to Abigail. The children in the school had news time every morning after they came in from their playtime break. They stood in front of the class to tell a piece of news. "And, Ivy's news was all about Aunt Elizabeth."

May sighed. "I miss the children's news."

The deacon stood to open the meeting in prayer, and the three young women stopped talking at once. Deborah had been so engrossed in talking that she hadn't noticed everybody had taken their seats.

WHEN THE MEETING WAS OVER, the three young women

were the last to walk out of the house and Andrew was waiting for Deborah on the porch. When Abigail and May noticed him there, they went ahead of Deborah to the food tables. Since they were the last ones out of the house, no one else was around.

In a low voice, Andrew said, "I think we should be seen together as much as possible, don't you?"

"I do. We'll just do what newly romantic couples normally do."

He put his hands on his hips and looked around with a silly grin on his face. "I feel everyone looking at us."

She gave a little giggle. "Me too."

"And, don't look over my shoulder now, but one of those people is William."

This was the best news Deborah could've hoped for. "Is that right?"

"*Jah.* He was looking at both of us just now trying to see what's going on."

"Is he jealous?"

Andrew smiled. "I think he could be."

"Oh, I just hope that this doesn't backfire in our faces."

"We'll just pretend like we're close friends, possibly courting, and then we can gradually drift apart when the right time comes."

"It sounds like you've done this kind of thing before."

He laughed. "Not likely. Now, are we in agreement that we're not going to tell anybody ever, right?"

"Of course not. People would think it's a dreadful thing to do."

He pulled a face. "It's not, but they might think that it is, I guess."

"Can I tell Aunt Agatha? She was the one who gave me the idea."

He looked around at Agatha. "Ah, she's talking to the bishop. I suppose you can tell her, but no one else."

"*Jah,* I think it would be safe to tell her. In fact, if she knew what was going on she might be able to help in some way."

"Why don't you sit down somewhere and I'll join you soon and bring you some food?" Andrew suggested.

"You don't know what kind I like."

"I'll just bring you a little bit of this and a little bit of that. A bit of everything."

"Okay."

He leaned closer, and whispered, "You never know, while I'm gone someone might sit with you."

Deborah nodded, but doubted that William Bronstein would. While Andrew made his way to the food table, she sat down by herself and then someone sat next to her. It was Aunt Agatha. "Have you taken my advice, Deborah?"

Deborah giggled. "I have. I was going to tell you soon, just you, because I don't want anybody else to know. Andrew has agreed to help me out and we're doing what you suggested."

"Good idea. Your secret's safe with me, and if this doesn't work, nothing will."

Deborah nodded. "That's exactly what I think. She glanced over at William, who was now sitting with his girls and Elizabeth, his sister. "I just hope things don't blow up in my face and go horribly wrong. I'm a teacher and I need to set a good example to my students."

"You're a person first and you have to do what's right for you. Your life's not teaching."

"Up until now it has been, for years now."

"It's about time you put that second place in your life and put other things first. You're not getting any younger you know."

Deborah grimaced. "That's something I don't need to be reminded of. I must be the oldest unmarried woman in the community." She didn't know one other Amish woman who was unmarried at thirty-three.

"Well, there are a few more, and these days —"

"I'm talking under the age of fifty, and who hasn't been widowed." At least the widows had once been married. Someone had wanted them.

"You're probably right." Aunt Agatha nodded. "What brings Andrew back?"

She didn't want to tell Aunt Agatha about Andrew's failed romance. It wasn't her news to tell. "He said he never went for good and ... he's back here now."

"Woman troubles, was it?"

She stared at Aunt Agatha hoping Andrew wouldn't think she had told her. "How did you know?"

"It's rather obvious when you look for the signs."

"What signs?"

Aunt Agatha chortled. "I'm teasing you. I've read all the Amish newspapers and I have several cousins who let me know what's what in the different communities. I know that Andrew was good friends with a young lady named Becky. Now her engagement's been announced and she's not marrying Andrew, she's marrying someone else. Now Andrew comes back here for no particular reason after he's been gone a number of years. I'm just joining the dots with the facts, that's all."

Slowly, Deborah nodded thinking that the older lady didn't need newspapers when she had all of her pen pals. "It's true. I feel very bad for him."

"*Jah*, me too. Unrequited love is so sad. Becky's getting married in December."

"It's awful for him and that's why he's so willing to help me."

Aunt Agatha pursed her lips. "At least you're benefiting from it."

"I guess so."

When Andrew got back to the table with two plates of food, Aunt Agatha rose to her feet. "Nice to see you again, Andrew."

"Nice to see you again too, Aunt Agatha. Looking after Deborah I see?"

"Of course."

"Would you like this plate of food? I can fetch myself another."

"I certainly will not disturb the two of you." She stood, and patted Andrew on the shoulder before she strode away.

Andrew sat down and picked up his knife and fork. "What did she want?"

"She guessed what's going on and I didn't even tell."

"That figures." He cut himself a piece of chicken and put it in his mouth.

In case other people knew about Becky, she had to tell him. "She also knew everything about you and Becky."

He nearly choked on his mouthful and had to cover his mouth with his hand. "How?"

"Pen pals. She's got cousins everywhere, it seems. And also, she saw Becky's wedding announcement in one of the Amish newspapers, she said."

"I suppose everybody will know. Maybe everybody does know. How do you think that looks for us and our plans?"

Feeling mischievous, Deborah leaned forward. "They might think you've left her for me."

A smile lit up his face. "Could be. I like the way you're thinking."

She looked down at the food. "Thanks for this."

"I hope I've found something you like amongst that."

"I'm not that fussy. I'll eat almost anything." She pushed some of the mashed potato into the coleslaw and then loaded a forkful. Before she put it into her mouth, she looked past Andrew to William. He was still sitting a few tables away from them.

Andrew waved a hand in front of her face, and whispered, "Stop looking at him."

"I'm not." Then she popped the food into her mouth.

"You are. And it won't be good if you're meant to be with me and he looks up and sees you looking at him."

"Good point."

Andrew cut up his chicken leg. "We've got to do this right."

"That's true. *Denke* for helping me. You're a true friend."

He smiled. "You just remember that for when I need a favor."

Not long after they finished eating, Andrew took Deborah home and then went back to his parents' house. Everybody would assume they were spending Sunday afternoon together and that was just what they wanted everyone to think.

CHAPTER 10

Deborah spent the whole school day on Monday hoping William would collect the children. When going-home time eventually came, she opened the door and was surprised that William's buggy was already there. William was leaning against it waiting. It was unusual for him to be there on time—more likely, he would be the last parent to arrive.

She stared back as the girls ran to him. Once they were sitting in the buggy, he walked over. Deborah had an inkling that her plan was unfolding just as she had hoped.

"I couldn't help but notice you and Andrew are spending a lot of time with one another."

"Jah, we are. We've always gotten along."

He pulled on the neckline of his shirt and looked uncomfortable. "I heard he was involved with some girl back in Sandy Creek."

"He was, but that's all finished with now."

He narrowed his eyes. "Are you sure about that?"

"I'm quite sure. That's what he told me and he wouldn't have said that if it wasn't true."

A smile spread across his face. "If you and he are only friends, would you come to dinner with the girls and me one night this week while Elizabeth is still here?"

Instantly, she felt she couldn't breathe and all words left her head. She tried to think quickly. If she accepted, he'd know she wasn't dating Andrew. Now she was in a bind. "Do you mean me by myself or with Andrew?"

When William chuckled, she had to wonder whether he knew about the charade.

Then one of the girls yelled to him trying to get his attention. He turned around to see they were now out of the buggy, and not only that, they were darting about playing tag. "Get back in the buggy, girls. I'll be there in a minute." They did as they were told, and he turned back to Deborah. "I happen to know he's been invited to Bishop Elmer's house on Tuesday night—tomorrow. So, how about tomorrow night for dinner?"

"You know more than I do, then."

He smiled. "I overheard it at the markets."

"Okay. I'd love to come for dinner and get to know your sister better. I've not really had a chance to talk with her."

"And I hope we'll all get to know you better, too."

She smiled, quite sure he knew nothing of the plan. "I'm sure there's not much to know." It seemed everything was working the way he was smiling at her like he'd never done before. Her cheeks were hot and she knew her face was beet red.

"I can't agree with that."

"What's that?" Deborah asked.

"I can't agree with the idea that there's not more to find out about you."

"Oh." She wanted to run away because of her blushing. It was a dead giveaway that she liked him.

"As long as you agree to come to dinner, that's all I can hope for today."

She nodded. "I'll look forward to it."

"Me too." He turned to leave, then turned back slightly. "Shall we make it at six o'clock at my place tomorrow?"

"That sounds good I'll be there at six."

He faced her more fully. *"Nee,* I'll collect you from your *haus* at six."

Shaking her head, she said, "There's no need to go to all that trouble."

"I'm adamant about it. I can't have you traveling alone in the streets at night."

She tilted her head. "I do it all the time."

"Not when you're coming to see me you don't, or you won't, I should say."

"If you insist."

"I do." He walked away, and then climbed up into his buggy. The girls waved to her.

"Bye, girls."

"Bye, Miss Deborah."

As always, Deborah waited until all the school children had been collected before she walked back into the schoolhouse.

CHAPTER 11

DEBORAH ARRIVED HOME a little later than usual and was just unhitching her buggy when Andrew pulled up beside her. She straightened up and waited for him to get out.

"Hello, Andrew. What's new?"

"Here, let me do that."

She moved aside and allowed him to finish the job she had started.

"*Mamm* said she was sorry, but she's developed a bad headache and is postponing dinner for another time."

Deborah had forgotten she'd been invited to a family dinner at Andrew's house. "That's fine, truly. Tell her I hope she'll feel better soon."

"She gets headaches from time to time. Bishop Elmer has invited me over to dinner tomorrow night. I was just there a few days ago."

"I know, I heard that. William told me this afternoon."

"How could he have known?"

She giggled. "He said he heard it at the markets. Anyway, I have some news of my own."

He frowned at her. "You've been invited too?"

"Nee, better than that. William Bronstein has asked me to dinner at his *haus* tomorrow night and he's collecting me and bringing me home again. Do you know how good that is?"

"I'm so happy for you."

"This is what I've wanted for years."

"It didn't take long for our plan to work."

"He said he heard you're going to Bishop Elmer's place for dinner and I think that's why he invited me the same night or something." She shrugged. "At first, I didn't know if I should refuse to go and have him think that it was because of you."

"Nee, you did the right thing. No need to make things too complicated. Things turned out good for you but not so good for me. I think there's some ulterior motive for the bishop asking me over there again. After dinner, he'll probably try to counsel me because he thinks I'm the guy who's gone from one relationship to the other. You know what the oversight is like about such things."

"If that's so, he's just worried about you, that's all."

Andrew sighed. "It sounds like you believe we're in a relationship."

"Nee." The idea made her laugh. "You're a wonderful friend, though."

"I don't think the bishop's worried about me at all. He might be worried about you getting involved with a character like me."

"Don't be silly; there's nothing wrong with you. I think you're looking on the downside of things."

He started giving her horse a rubdown. "I might have time for a quick *kaffe*. How about you make me one while I do this?"

"That sounds like a fair exchange. I'll see you in the kitchen, and the horse just goes through that gate there."

He nodded. "Gotcha."

She walked into the kitchen feeling pleased with the amount of male attention she was getting lately. After she took off her black coat and traveling bonnet, she headed to the kitchen with them under her arm to place them on the hook by the back door.

Already, she was a bundle of nerves about the dinner tomorrow night. She wiped her hands on a nearby hand towel before she looked out the window at Andrew. *Gott* had sent him along at the very right time. She hoped things would work out well for him too, and in time, he would find somebody that he liked as much as Becky.

When Andrew came into the kitchen, she was just placing two mugs of coffee onto the table. "Good timing." She pulled out a chair and sat down.

"Where can I wash?" He held his hands in the air.

"Ah, just through there." She pointed to the laundry room just off from the kitchen.

When he came back, he sat opposite and picked up his coffee mug. "You must be very excited about tomorrow night."

"I am, I mean, I will be when I get over the shock. I still can't believe it. And he's going to collect me and bring me back too."

He smiled at her and then wrapped both his hands around the coffee mug. "Thanks for this."

"You're welcome. That's the least I could do when you've done so much to help me."

Andrew rolled his eyes. "Just think of me tomorrow night at Bishop Elmer's *haus.* I hope his talk with me isn't going to be too stern."

"Just tell him we're only friends because that's the truth of it. Anyway, Becky is getting married, so even if we were boyfriend and girlfriend I don't see what the harm would be. Perhaps you should tell your parents your announcement to them was a little hasty?"

"Who knows?" He stared into his coffee. When he took a sip, he placed it back down on the table and looked up at her. "What is this?"

"Coffee."

"I'm not so sure about that."

"It's just a blend I get from the markets. Don't you like it?" She knew he didn't approve. It had been the cheapest coffee she could find.

He raised his eyebrows and took another sip. "I'm not sure what I think of it."

When he pulled another face, she giggled. "You don't have to be polite. It's just coffee. I won't be upset if you don't like it. I just won't offer you another mug."

"I'll bring you some of my favorite coffee for you to try. I brought some with me. I'm not sure if you can get it around here."

"You brought coffee all the way from Sandy Creek?"

He nodded. "I did. Is that strange?"

"Nee, not at all. Not if you really like that coffee."

"I do. I drink some in the morning first thing and then I don't drink it again all day unless I have a small cup after dinner. Or, if I have some when I'm visiting folks."

"So, you pretty much have *kaffe* whenever, all through the day?"

He laughed. "Maybe."

"I'll remember that. I would very much like to try some of your special coffee."

"If things turn out well for you tomorrow night, we not might not be spending much time together. You'll have to tell William we're just friends."

"That'll be the truth because we are just friends."

"I realize that, but I'm pretty sure William thought things might be moving in a different direction with the two of us and that's why he made his move."

"Ah, and you think it's best I set his thinking right tomorrow night?"

"It's important that you do."

She looked down into her hot drink. "You're right about the coffee. It sort of tastes like nothing, and when you swallow a mouthful, there's no nice lingering coffee flavor."

He nodded. "It's pretty dreadful. I didn't want to offend you by saying so."

"I don't drink much coffee when I'm at home. I like to have it when I go out though."

He smiled at her, and then asked, "Will William's *schweschder* be there tomorrow night?"

"*Jah,* she will. I don't even know her very well. It will be good to know more about her. I should've introduced you to her on Sunday."

"Do you know anything about her?"

"All I know is her husband's been ill and she's been looking after him for three years. He needed constant care, but I heard he was doing better. I guess someone else must be looking after him now to enable her to get away to see her *bruder* and her nieces."

"I'm happy for you that everything's worked so quickly."

"It hasn't 'worked' yet. It's just dinner."

"The rest is up to you."

She sighed. "I hope he likes me enough."

"Of course he will. Why wouldn't he? He'd be a fool if he didn't."

She giggled. *"Denke."* When he sighed deeply, she asked, "What is it?"

He looked across at her. "We were good friends when we were younger, so why didn't things work out for us back then?"

She thought back in time for a moment and then stared into his hazel eyes. "I guess some people are just meant to be friends and nothing more. Besides, you left for Sandy Creek when you were nineteen without a second thought for me."

He laughed. "I did, but I don't think you were pining after me either." He pushed the coffee away from him just slightly. "Do you mind if I don't drink any more of this?"

"That bad, is it?"

He nodded.

"Can I make you a hot tea instead?"

"Nee, denke. I should get home and help *Dat* with the dinner anyway." He stood up.

"I hope your *mudder* gets better soon."

He nodded as he walked to the door. "Me too."

"Thanks for all you've done, Andrew."

He stopped still and turned back. "That sounds like a goodbye."

"Definitely not."

He smiled at her. "I'll stop by Wednesday afternoon, if you don't mind, and find out how things went for you at the dinner."

"I'll look forward to it and you can tell me about dinner with the bishop."

He rubbed his chin. "I hope it's not going to be too bad."

"Of course it won't be. He hasn't seen you for years. He probably just wants to catch up, that's all."

"He saw me only last week. I stopped by out of politeness to let him know that I'm back for a while. That's why I think someone's said something."

"Maybe."

When Andrew turned back toward the door to go, she walked outside with him feeling bad that things were working out well for her and Andrew looked so sad.

CHAPTER 12

TUESDAY WAS JUST LIKE any other typical school day yet Deborah was full of butterflies thinking about the man she'd loved for years. It didn't seem real that she was finally going to be included in one of his family dinners especially with his sister visiting. That made it even more critical that she make a good impression. Ivy and Grace were excited about her coming to dinner and talked of little else at school. They loved Deborah and she loved them right back. It would be perfect to have those children as her own to raise, and she knew she would be an excellent wife to William.

When school was over and William stepped out of his buggy to greet the children, she noticed he seemed distracted and had trouble looking her in the face. Had he changed his mind before she even had dinner at his house? In her heart, she knew something was wrong.

"William, if you don't want me to come tonight I don't have to." She always found the straightforward approach was best. Even though she'd be disappointed, it would save her pain and things wouldn't be dragging out over an awful dinner. She'd already had one dinner with him like that and wasn't looking forward to another.

He looked up at her, smiled and then chuckled. "I'm sorry if I seem distracted. I've been having problems with a fellow at work, but it's nothing that can't be solved. It's nothing to do with you. That's been the bright spot in my day, you having dinner with us tonight."

She gave an inward sigh of relief. That's what she had wanted to hear.

Ivy said, "Come on, *Dat.* I told Aunt Elizabeth I'd be there to help her with the dinner."

"I'm coming," he called over his shoulder as the two girls climbed into the buggy.

As soon as they were in, Deborah heard the girls arguing over something. William rolled his eyes. "Here we go again. They're squabbling over who's going to do what with the dinner."

"It sounds like more of a lively negotiation to me."

Her comment made him laugh. "Only someone kind like yourself would make excuses for them. What's squabbling to me is a negotiation to you."

She bit her lip. Was he thinking they were too different already before things had even begun? Her mind wouldn't stop going to negative places.

"I should get them home to help with the dinner and I'll be at your place at six?"

She nodded. "I'll be ready, and I'm looking forward to it."

"Me too." He took two steps back still smiling at her.

She knew there was something different between them and it filled her heart with gladness.

When the schoolhouse and grounds were deserted Deborah made her way home. If she'd known what would've made William notice her, she would've done it a long time ago.

To the rhythmic sound of the horse's hooves, she fell into a trance-like state imagining her wedding when she married William. She'd wear a brand-new dark blue dress with sheer white organza cape, *kapp* and apron. William would look fine in a dark suit that she'd sewn for him. Tasting all the wedding cakes before she decided on which ones to include, mmm, that would be a treat, and she'd take May with her. May was fond of cake too. Even though the ladies in the community always made some of the cakes for a wedding breakfast most often the bride's family bought cakes too.

After she planned the wedding clothes, and the wedding breakfast, she imagined living in William's house and how she would change things to make it more like her own. Surely, he wouldn't mind her making a few alterations—otherwise, it would feel like it was still William's late wife's home, too. *And wouldn't that feel awkward?* she mused. To keep the children included, they'd help her make the changes. They could also help her make new curtains and if they didn't already know how to knit, she'd show them so they could knit clothes for all their new brothers and sisters.

Now looking up at the gray sky, she wondered if she'd miss running the school.

She shook her head. *Nee, I won't.*

There would be no comparison. Marriage to William and becoming a mother was all she'd dreamed of. With May being a newlywed, maybe she'd have to look for a new woman to help out with the teaching. The board hadn't said anything, yet, but she wondered. Of course, if she married soon—as she hoped—the board would soon be finding replacements for the both of them.

She laughed at herself when she realized she'd made a life plan for the next five years, when William had never even mentioned marriage and they weren't even courting.

Her future hung on how tonight turned out. If she didn't get along with Elizabeth, William would not take things further with her. More than anything, it was important she get on well with Elizabeth tonight. Perhaps even more so than getting along with William.

She knew how important a woman's opinion was in a man's life and now that William's—and Elizabeth's—parents were gone, he'd respect his older sister and her judgment. Thinking about Elizabeth caused her mind to wander some more. With Elizabeth's husband so ill, would they end up having her living with William and her? It would be just like Rebecca having Anne living with them. Anne often looked after young Micah, Rebecca's stepson, so Rebecca could continue her midwifery work.

Deborah scolded herself for thinking that way. Elizabeth's husband was in recovery, and here she was making plans for after his demise.

Her mind was racing at a million miles per minute and she couldn't help it. She was a planner and liked to have her life mapped out before her, but doing that would raise her hopes.

Andrew came into her mind. He was a good friend and her mother had always told her that a husband should also be your best friend. William wasn't her best friend, not yet, and she could definitely say that even though Andrew had been missing in her life for years, he'd quickly resumed his role as her confidant.

Despite what her mother had said, she couldn't see herself married to Andrew, but she could definitely see herself married to William. The butterflies in her stomach weren't there for Andrew like they were there every time she thought about William. It was important to her that she have that giddy romantic love for the man she was to marry.

Deborah knew she was no beauty and it never really bothered her. What mattered was that somebody liked her for the person she was inside, not outside. Then she remembered—William had said he was looking forward to getting to know her better tonight.

When Deborah got home, she stilled those pesky butterflies in her stomach, showered, and then changed into her best dress. Just as she tied the apron strings behind her back, she glanced at the clock in the kitchen. There was an hour to fill in before six o'clock.

Figuring she needed to do something to take her mind off her nerves, she retrieved a long-forgotten sampler and started sewing. What seemed like three hours later rather than one, she finally heard the sounds of a horse's hooves and buggy wheels crunching the small pebbles on her driveway. At once, the nerves kicked in again, and in a hurry to put her sampler away, she managed to jab the needle into her finger. "Ouch! she blurted, and then a drop of blood landed on her white apron.

"Oh, bother." It was the nicest one she owned and the only other clean one was old. Without wasting a moment, she squeezed her thumb against the wound to stop the bleeding, whisked off the apron with her other hand, hurried to the kitchen and held the soiled section under the cold running water. The spot was soon gone, but in its place was a dark wet patch. It looked awful. Then there was the problem that her finger was still bleeding. She laid the apron aside and decided to wear the older one and just as she was running her finger under cold water, a knock sounded on the door. "I'm coming," she called out.

Shaking her finger dry, she pulled open the bottom drawer with the other hand and pulled out a length of bandaging gauze and wrapped it firmly around her finger. In the laundry room, she found the clean but unironed apron. The night was off to a bad start.

When she finally opened the door to William, she held up her bandaged finger. "Sorry to keep you waiting, but I stuck my finger with a needle."

He pulled a face. "Why would you do that?"

She giggled. "It wasn't on purpose. I was sewing and I don't know how I did it but I managed to stab myself. Then it bled onto my only clean, ironed apron." Looking down at herself, she said, "I hope Elizabeth doesn't think I'm an untidy person. If you have time, I can press this one."

He smiled at her. "If you hadn't had told me, I would never have noticed and I'm sure it won't bother Elizabeth."

"It'll only take a minute, or two."

"Nee, no need; you look fine to me."

That was the best thing he could have said.

"Ready?" he asked.

"Jah. I'll just turn off some lights." She left one lamp on in the living room so she could see when she got back home. Once she had shut the front door, she noticed the look on his face. "What's wrong?"

"Won't you be cold?"

"Ach, jah, I forgot my coat." She opened the door just enough to reach her hand through and grab the coat from the peg by the door. She flipped the coat around her shoulders rather than putting it on properly and then they walked to the buggy. Once they'd climbed in, she said, "I feel awful for keeping you waiting."

He sat beside her and smiled warmly. "I thought you might keep me waiting. Most women take their time."

"Not me. I like to be punctual. I'm mostly early. I got into that habit a long time ago, even before I start teaching. My *vadder* taught me it was selfish to make others wait for me."

"That's good to know." He walked the horse to the middle of the driveway and then click him forward. "The girls are so excited about you coming to dinner. They've been cooking with Elizabeth since they arrived home."

"I hope they haven't gone to too much trouble."

"They're having fun. They're enjoying a company of another female around the place. They haven't had that for a while."

"Jah, it's been a while now that ... Oh, I'm sorry. I

shouldn't talk about her. It'll only make you upset." Now she felt like an idiot.

"That's fine. Nita's always in my life, every day, even though I'm well aware she's gone home to *Gott*. Every time I look at my two girls, I see her smiling back at me."

This was going horribly wrong. In the first two minutes they were alone, they were talking about his late wife and his devotion to her. She had to change the subject. "The girls are doing well in school." With a curious expression on his face, he glanced over at her. Then she knew the change had been too drastic. "I just thought you should know."

"That's good. I was worried about Grace before she started school. I thought she might be a little bit young and would have trouble keeping up with the other children. Mary and Samuel held their *dochder* a year and I often wonder if I did the right thing sending her to school, but there was really no one to look after her during the day."

"Worry is a common thing amongst parents. They always worry if they're doing the right thing or not. I wouldn't be concerned. She's managing just fine and it helps to have Ivy there with her. How do you think you'll manage with that problem at work?"

"What's that?"

"Today, you said you were worried about someone at work." She knew she was jumping from one subject to another like a flea jumping about on a dog but after the other night at Aunt Agatha's, she wanted to keep the conversation flowing and that was the only way she knew to do it.

"Ah that. That will sort itself out soon enough. Elizabeth might be collecting the girls from school every now and again while she's here."

"How long is she staying?"

"Probably another week, maybe more. Her husband has ordered her to stay away for a while until she has had a good break. His sickness has taken a toll on her."

"He's recovering, isn't he?"

"That's right."

"That's good." Deborah didn't say anything but she could see for herself that Elizabeth had spent several years with stress and sleeplessness. She looked years older than she should.

CHAPTER 13

When they arrived at William's house, the door opened and Elizabeth stood on the porch with Ivy on one side and Grace on the other. They were smiling and Deborah knew from the pleasant expression on Elizabeth's face she would have a good evening. If Elizabeth was as nice as Nancy, William's other sister, all would be well. William walked her to the door and once she'd greeted everyone, he went back to care for his horse.

Ivy said, "We've been cooking and we've been a good help. Haven't we?" Ivy looked up at her Aunt Elizabeth.

"*Jah*, you've both been an excellent help. I don't think I could have done it without you both."

Ivy and Grace giggled at the compliment.

"Mmm. I can smell some *wunderbaar* food," Deborah said.

Elizabeth moved the girls away from the door. "Come in out of the cold, Deborah."

As she walked into the house, Grace said, "I helped make the applesauce."

"We helped with everything, didn't we, Aunt Elizabeth?" Ivy asked.

"That's right. They'll make good *fraas* one day."

The girls huddled together giggling.

"Is there anything I can help with, Elizabeth? I wanted to bring something, but William wouldn't allow it."

Elizabeth shook her head. "Everything's under control. We'll sit here in the living room for a few minutes and get to know each other, shall we?"

"Sounds good."

"Girls, why don't you go up to your room and play for a few minutes?"

The girls weren't so happy with that suggestion. "Do we have to?" Ivy asked.

"*Jah,* you do."

Grace said, "I want to stay and talk to Miss Deborah."

Ivy took a hold on Grace's sleeve. "Come on, Grace. It's no use." The girls headed up the stairs.

"They're so well behaved," Deborah commented.

"Mainly, they are. And might I ask you, Deborah, what's happening between you and my *bruder?* This is the first time I've heard about you."

That was what she had feared. He'd never mentioned her other than in her capacity as a teacher, if he'd mentioned her at all. "There's nothing to tell. He's just asked me to come here for dinner. I'm the girls' teacher. Oh, that's right you know that already."

"Is that all?"

Deborah shrugged her shoulders. "That's all." Deborah

gave a little giggle and couldn't blame Elizabeth for asking. If she had a brother she'd be the first to inquire if he brought a woman to dinner.

"Are you fond of William?" Elizabeth asked.

"He's a good man. I am fond of him."

"I can see you're friends, but you'd like to be more?"

One question was fine, but now she was probing too far. "Tell me more about you, Elizabeth. There were so many people surrounding you on Sunday I didn't get a chance to speak with you."

"Oh, there's not much to tell. My *kinner* have all left home and my dear husband has been ill for some years."

"I heard about that, and you're here having a bit of a vacation—time to rejuvenate?"

"I am, it's true."

"Can I ask what's wrong with him?"

"David had a sudden stroke and was paralyzed down one side and couldn't do much of anything for himself."

"Oh, I'm sorry to hear it."

"He has improved a lot. He's able to walk now, and do some things without help, and that's why I'm taking this opportunity to visit William. My cousin is staying there to look after him."

"That's good of her."

"Him. He's James." Elizabeth corrected. "The two of them have always been as close as brothers. James is looking after him now."

"That's good. I'm glad you got the chance to get away."

"Me too."

William walked through the door.

"William, come sit with us," Elizabeth called out.

He looked around as he sat down. "Where are the girls?"

"I sent them to their rooms, so we can have an adult conversation without little ears listening in."

A small smile spread across William's face. "I think I don't get enough adult conversation. At work it's pretty much all business."

"That's something you should try to get more of, real conversation," said Elizabeth.

"I'll keep that in mind."

"Deborah, William was telling me earlier today how he doesn't have much time with adults now that he's the sole parent of his children."

"Yes, everybody needs some adult conversation every now and again. I know when I get home after a long day I sometimes crave an adult to converse with."

Elizabeth looked from Deborah to William. "Perhaps you would both find a benefit from more of each other's company?"

William smiled and Deborah gave an embarrassed giggle. Having his sister as an ally surely wouldn't hurt, but this seemed to be moving rather fast.

She looked across at William and he didn't seem to mind what Elizabeth had said because he was smiling at her.

"Maybe we should. That could be an excellent idea of yours, Elizabeth," William said.

Immediately, Elizabeth jumped to her feet. "If you'll excuse me, I'll see how far away dinner is."

When she left the room, he leaned across, and whispered, "I'm sorry about that. She's always trying to marry me off."

Deborah went from elated to disappointed with that one comment. "You've got nothing to be sorry about. She's just concerned for you and the girls."

"We're fine as we are."

Deborah nodded. "You're doing well."

"Of course we're doing well," William said, and then he surprised her by adding, "That's not to say that the situation couldn't be improved."

She gulped, and all her nervousness returned—a lump formed in her throat and the butterflies were nearly making her sick.

"I'm a very forthright person and there's something I need to ask you, Deborah."

Deborah froze. Was he going to propose right now, there in his house with his daughters and sister present? She swallowed hard against the lump in her throat, and somehow found her voice. "Go on."

"What is your relationship to Andrew? I saw you arrive with him for the meeting."

"Andrew and I are just friends—long-time friends."

His eyebrows rose. "Sometimes friendships develop into ... something else?"

She didn't want to reassure him too much that Andrew and she were only friends, especially now when it seemed Aunt Agatha's plan was working. "Well I don't know too much about love."

"You don't?"

She laughed and couldn't deceive him further, so she

playfully added, "I'll let you know when things have progressed from friendship, okay?"

"I hope they never do. I'm hoping you and I might spend a little more time together, seeing Elizabeth is here to watch the girls."

"Really?"

"Jah. Would you?"

"Jah, I'd like that very much."

"Why don't we do something this coming Saturday?"

Her Saturdays were usually spent washing laundry, and doing housekeeping chores and all the other things she couldn't get to during the week. "I don't think I have any plans for then."

"Good; now you do."

They smiled at one another and she knew at that moment that the attraction was mutual–finally. As though she'd been listening in on their conversation, Elizabeth came back into the room.

"I'll go upstairs and get the girls. Dinner is nearly ready to be served."

Deborah jumped to her feet. "Can I do anything?"

"Stay there. The girls and I will serve and then we'll call you when we're ready for you to sit down at the table." Elizabeth hurried past them and then headed up the stairs. Just seconds later, the girls bounded down the stairs in front of Elizabeth. "Walk!" The girls slowed their pace to a fast walk.

CHAPTER 14

SOON THEY SAT down to dinner, the first one of many that Deborah hoped to have at William's house. They closed their eyes and said their individual silent prayers of thanks for the food. After that, the food was passed around.

"This looks delicious," Deborah said.

Elizabeth grinned. "I hope it tastes delicious."

"My sister is an amazing cook."

"Do you like cooking, Deborah?" Elizabeth asked.

"I do, but I don't have anyone to cook for, living by myself. I would like a reason to do more of it."

"What kind of a reason?" Ivy asked.

"Did anyone ask you anything?" Elizabeth asked Ivy.

Deborah felt sorry for Ivy when she saw the crushed look of sadness on her face. She recalled exactly how she had felt as a child, continually being shushed by adults while at the dinner table. "Having more people to cook for. That's what I meant, Ivy," Deborah answered.

Ivy's mouth turned up into a slight smile.

Deborah popped a bite of pork into her mouth, chewed and swallowed. "Oh, this is amazing."

"There's a special way I cook it."

"Would you tell me?" Deborah asked.

"Of course. Our *mudder* always used to cook pork this way. The secret is a lower temperature than what most people would cook it at, but first, partially braising it before cooking. I'll write out the recipe for you."

"That would be *wunderbaar, denke.*"

"What have you girls made for dessert?" William asked.

"A cherry cake," answered Elizabeth. "It was *Mamm's* speciality wasn't it, William?"

William smiled and nodded.

Deborah was pleased that Elizabeth was cooking some of their mother's favorite and special recipes rather than using those from William's late wife because that would've been awkward.

As DEBORAH MUNCHED her way through the wonderfully rich German cherry cake with its tart cherries, dark chocolate, and cream frosting, she could feel William's gaze upon her. She looked up to see him smiling at her. She could tell without a doubt that he liked her. When she smiled back at him it was as though they had a secret all their very own.

After dinner, the girls started to clear the table and Elizabeth said, "I will make the two of you some tea. Go and sit out in the living room."

Together, Deborah and William made their way into the living room.

"I'm feeling very spoiled," Deborah said.

"Elizabeth is certainly a good cook."

"She sure is. That cake was amazing. Did your *mudder* make the cake as well as that?"

"I don't think that's possible. Elizabeth has perfected *Mamm's* recipes over time. Nancy has too."

"It would be nice to have the time to experiment with recipes."

He nodded. "I hope you get that opportunity."

"Maybe someday." They weren't alone for long before Elizabeth brought a tray of tea items in and set it on the table before them. The girls walked in behind Elizabeth, Ivy carrying cookies and Grace with a small plate of chocolate treats.

"*Denke,* Elizabeth, and girls. We're having a feast tonight," Deborah said.

"Aunt Elizabeth would not let us carry in the hot drinks. She said we were too young."

Deborah nodded. "That's right, but you'll soon be old enough to carry hot cups."

"Maybe in a couple of years," William said.

They all sat and talked for a while, even the children.

When it was time for the children to go to bed, Deborah was invited to accompany William up the stairs to say good night.

This was the best thing that could happen and the night had turned out just as she had hoped. He'd have to drive her home, just the two of them, while Elizabeth stayed behind to watch the girls.

When they headed back down the stairs together, he said, "Are you ready to go now?"

"*Jah*, whenever you're ready."

He called out to his sister and told her that they were leaving. Elizabeth came out of the kitchen. "*Denke* for coming, Deborah. It was a delightful night. We all enjoyed your company, especially the girls."

"I had a *wunderbaar* time, and I haven't had food that good for as long as I can remember. *Denke.*" Deborah walked to the door behind William.

Elizabeth followed her. "I hope I'll be seeing a lot more of you."

"Me too. Do you know when you're going home?"

"*Nee.* I call my cousin every day to see how my husband is. He's doing fine and will be doing fine as long as his cousin is able to stay with him. I'm guessing it will be a few more days, no longer."

William opened the door while handing Deborah her coat. "You ready?"

"I am." She turned around and hugged Elizabeth good-bye. "I'll see you soon."

"It'll likely be me collecting the children tomorrow."

"Okay, I'll see you then."

She walked out with William and climbed into the buggy. Then he walked around and climbed up next to her and they headed down the road.

"It's nice to see someone getting along with my sister."

That surprised Deborah. "I'm sure she would get along with everyone."

He chuckled. "I don't know about that. She has been a bit withdrawn from social settings these last few years."

"She's having a well-needed break with you."

"She seems to be relaxing more. And she enjoyed your company tonight I could tell."

"Denke for tonight."

He glanced over at Deborah. "It's me who should be thanking you. I hope you come again."

"Of course I will. Or you could come to my *haus* and try out my cooking, but don't expect it to be as good as Elizabeth's."

He chuckled "It's the company that's important and not the food so much."

"How about next week?"

"For dinner?"

"Jah."

"You name the day and we'll be there."

Deborah was pleased to hear it. "Okay. I'll work it out and let you know when I see you next."

"I will try my very best to talk Elizabeth out of collecting the girls tomorrow. I look forward to our conversations of an afternoon."

"You do?"

"I do—and I kind of thought you might too," William said with a questioning tone of voice.

"Oh, I do. I just wasn't sure that you did … I do. Very much so."

"Are you sure about doing something with me on Saturday? I'm not stepping on somebody's toes?"

"Nee, you wouldn't be. I'm looking forward to a lovely time."

"Elizabeth should still be here, and she can look after the girls so we can have some quiet time." He chuckled.

"They do like to chatter. It's a hard balance knowing how much to keep them quiet or let them speak."

"It must be difficult to judge. It'll be just the two of us then?"

"*Jah*, if that's all right by you?" He turned to face her.

"I'd like that very much."

"I always knew there was something special about you, Deborah."

He'd taken his time to show it. "You did?" She bit the inside of her lip wishing she could have found a more intelligent response—being a teacher, especially—but it was too late now.

"*Jah*. I've been thinking about you for a long time and I was hoping you might feel the same about me."

This was her time to show him she had feelings too. It was not the time to play games. "I admit I have been thinking about you too." Happiness flooded her body. This was the best thing that could've happened, and she had to thank Aunt Agatha for her brilliant idea. Also, her dear friend, Andrew, had played a part in prompting William to reveal his innermost feelings.

He glanced at her. "I'm happy to hear it."

They traveled the rest of the journey in silence, but this time it wasn't that awkward kind of silence, it was a pleasant one. They had both admitted their feelings and there was a feeling of harmony and completeness.

Then William placed the reins in one hand and turned to Deborah. "I must tell you, I've had a *wunderbaar* time with you just now."

"I'm glad, and I've enjoyed it, too."

"Good. We're both adults above a certain age. You're a

mature woman, I'm a mature man and we get along well together and I'm pretty certain we think along the same lines about everything that matters."

She smiled and nodded, wishing she could add something intelligent to the conversation, but nothing came to mind so she stayed quiet, hoping the conversation was leading somewhere important.

"What I'm trying to say to you, Deborah, is that I'm not wasting your time. I would like more than anything to marry again. That's where this is heading."

She smiled again. "That's good to know and I never thought for one moment that you were wasting my time."

"I'm hoping I might be the type of man you want to marry."

"You are."

"Thank you for taking the time to get to know me. I feel flattered you're willing to spend time with me."

"You're flattered?" Too soon for a proposal, he was openly telling her of his intentions.

"*Jah*, I am," he said.

"I never really thought you'd be interested in a woman like me."

He chuckled. "What kind of woman did you think I'd be interested in?"

"I'm not sure but you'd have a lot of options open to you. You're as perfect a man as *Gott* created, I'm sure of it."

He threw his head back and laughed. "I'm far from perfect and you will be disappointed if you think that, when you learn of my downside. Everyone has faults and flaws. I'm not sure if you do, but most people in the world do." He smiled at her as he gave her the compliment.

"I agree everyone has flaws, but I hope you don't find out about mine too soon."

He laughed again. "I'm sure if they exist they're very minor indeed."

"Maybe." They arrived back at her house and she hoped he'd stay awhile. "Come inside for coffee or something before you go?"

"I better get back to my girls. We'll talk more about this on Saturday."

"Oh yes, of course." She got out of the buggy and just as she reached her porch, she turned around. "Bye, William."

"I'll see you soon, Deborah."

When he drove away, she opened the door feeling like she was floating. He'd said marriage was on his mind— that was the best thing she could have heard. After she kicked off her shoes, she slumped into the couch and closed her eyes, dreaming of a lifetime with William and his two girls, and then all the children she and William would have together.

She was sure he wouldn't delay things too much and she hoped they'd marry by Christmas. And quite possibly her wedding might be the next one announced. There was no greater feeling. Everybody would be so excited when they found out. She closed her eyes and thanked God for blessing her so quickly. No man had ever liked her or said the things to her that William had. This was what she had been waiting for all of her life.

She could now, for the first time, see marriage to William as a reality. After she got up and hung up her coat, she walked over and fell onto the lounge, lying back as she closed her eyes. She'd wanted to be a mother for so long, and that was what had prompted her to say yes when the school board approached her. She had thought that if she couldn't have her own *kinner*, she'd be close to children by teaching them.

The school board preferred teachers to be unmarried and free of distractions other than their pupils. She made up her mind that after school tomorrow she would go to Aunt Agatha's house and give her an update on how well her ingenious plan had worked. Then she'd have to figure out what to cook for William and his family when they came for dinner.

Knowing she had to come up with something different and yet special, she hurried to the kitchen and pulled down her mother's recipe file and leafed through the cards filled with handwritten recipes. She was sure William would appreciate food that wasn't too fancy; plain yet wholesome. When she found a couple of possibilities, she set those cards aside and put the other recipes away.

CHAPTER 15

THE NEXT DAY, all Deborah could think about was seeing William after school. She could barely hide her disappointment when she wandered over to William's buggy and saw Elizabeth sitting in the front seat. The only thing she could do was fix a smile upon her face.

"William had to work," was the first thing Elizabeth told her.

Deborah smiled and made the necessary polite conversation while doing her best to hide the unavoidable disappointment. She cheered up when she remembered she would have his undivided attention on Saturday. Besides, he had admitted he was interested in her and that was a huge step forward.

After Deborah locked up the schoolhouse, she made her way to Aunt Agatha's. When Aunt Agatha opened her front door, flanked by two cats, Deborah smiled. *"Denke."*

"For what?"

"Your plan worked."

Aunt Agatha's face lit up. "You'd better come inside and let me know what happened. I need to hear everything from start to finish." Aunt Agatha led her into the kitchen where she had just made a fresh pot of tea. "Tea?"

"*Jah,* please."

Aunt Agatha sat in front of her, poured the tea, and then pushed the cup and saucer toward her. "Now, what happened from the beginning?"

She proceeded to tell her all about the dinner with the girls and Elizabeth. "And, Elizabeth is lovely, and her cooking was delicious."

"I'm not asking about delicious, I want to know more about what happened with William."

Deborah giggled. "Oh, I get a bit embarrassed talking about it."

"Tell me. I deserve that, don't I?"

"*Jah,* you do. We're spending the whole of Saturday together while Elizabeth is looking after his girls." Deborah took a sip of tea and then placed the cup carefully down onto the saucer. "He mentioned marriage. He didn't ask me, but he did say that's where we were heading."

Aunt Agatha's face beamed. "Good. We made him jealous and then he realized he didn't want to lose you. He might've if he'd taken any longer."

Deborah nibbled on the end of her fingernail. "I know he's an earnest man. I only hope he never finds out about me fooling him."

"You didn't. You just spent some time with a male friend. Anyway, he won't find out—and anyway, what would be the harm?"

Deborah shook her head. "I know him well enough to know that he wouldn't like it. He's very set in his ways about things."

Aunt Agatha sighed. "It seems that's a risk you'll have to take."

"I guess so. Otherwise, if he hadn't seen me with Andrew, none of this might ever have happened." She knew Aunt Agatha was right.

"It seems we'll have another wedding coming soon."

"Me?" Deborah asked.

Aunt Agatha nodded and then jumped with fright when a cat jumped into her lap. "Not at the table, Sooty." She pushed the black cat off her and he meowed something that sounded like disapproval. Looking back at Deborah, Agatha said, "You and William will be next to be married. That's my guess."

"I just wouldn't be able to believe it if it happened. Do you think so?"

"Of course. Why else would you be going out somewhere with him on Saturday? I wouldn't be surprised if he proposes to you on Saturday. Widowers don't waste their time finding a second wife. That's what I've noticed."

Deborah giggled. That would be her dream come true. "I hope so, but it would be taking things a little quick and William is different from most men."

"In my long experience over my many years on *Gott's* green earth, they're all the same."

Deborah had to giggle. "That's true, I guess he's the same in some ways but different in others."

"It doesn't matter. He just needed a bit of a shakeup, that's all."

"Anyway, I wanted to say a big thank you."

"You don't need to thank me. He would've realized you were right for him sooner or later."

"I'm only glad it was sooner. It feels like I have waited long enough. I've been teaching his girls for years. And we've talked nearly every day after school."

ON THE WAY home from Aunt Agatha's house, she saw Andrew's buggy approaching. She could tell it was his horse pulling the buggy because his family's bay buggy horse had one white sock. They both slowed their horses and stopped in the middle of the road. "Where are you off to?" she asked him.

"I was coming to see you, but you weren't home. I was going for a drive before I headed home again."

"I was just speaking to Aunt Agatha, but I'm on my way home now. Follow me back and I'll make you a cup of coffee and tell you the news."

"Just as well I came prepared." He lifted up a bag of coffee and showed her.

She giggled. "Good. That should save me from your complaining. We can try it out."

"It'll be much better than the coffee you've been giving me. Trust me."

CHAPTER 16

Several minutes later, Deborah and Andrew sat in her kitchen waiting for the water to boil. She told Andrew everything that had happened between her and William.

"Well, that didn't take long." Andrew leaned back in his chair.

"How long did you think it would take?"

"I'm not sure. I didn't think it would be as fast as that."

"I can't tell you how pleased I am to be spending the whole day with him Saturday.

"More pleased than when we spent the day together on Saturday, this last Saturday?"

She looked at him wondering if he was a little jealous. "Well, that was a little different, don't you think?"

"Because you're in love with William and not in love with me?"

She frowned at him. "We're just friends."

"That's a good thing, though. The best relationships are built on friendships."

"Have you forgotten about Becky so quickly?"

He shook his head. "Don't talk to me about her. It seems I was always meant to be alone." His shoulders slumped and she could feel his black mood.

"Don't be like that. That's what I thought and then all of a sudden everything came together. I'm sure William and I will be courting after Saturday."

"Don't get me wrong. I'm happy for you. As happy for you as I would be if something good happened for myself, however unlikely that might be."

"Don't be like that. May's wedding is in a couple of days. I'm sure you'll meet someone there. People come from all over the place. You never know who's going to be there."

He nodded. "You're not the first person to mention that I might find a lovely girl at May's wedding." He rolled his eyes. "I told *Mamm* you and I aren't a real … that we're not in a relationship. That got you out of having to come for dinner."

"Oh, I see."

"She was disappointed–she really likes you, I guess. Then she started going on and on about May's wedding. As if I want to hear about a wedding knowing I should've married Becky."

"You must believe and have faith that someone else will come along."

"You're right, but I must admit it's hard to keep believing when all you see is things not turning out right. Look, I don't mean to depress you when you're so happy. I'm happy for you, I'm just miserable for myself."

"I know how you feel. I was like that and now things

are working out. It might take time, but it will happen. It might happen for you quickly just like it did for me."

"That is something I find hard to believe.

She felt so sorry for him. "It's true."

He nodded. "It just seems unbelievable to me, that's all."

"I didn't have anyone and now I do. It happened overnight, in the blink of an eye. That's why I know things are going to work out for you."

He smiled and nodded. "How's that *kaffe?*" He nodded to the kettle that was whistling.

She jumped to her feet and took the kettle off the stove. "Let's see if I can make you a decent cup of *kaffe.*"

"*Jah*, that would be a first."

They both laughed. "I have a coffee plunger; it doesn't make it as lovely as those fancy machines in the cafés."

"The plunger will be fine. You'll see, the *kaffe* will taste a lot better than what you've given me before."

She poured the ground coffee into the hot water and let it sit for a while.

"Don't let it get too cold. I like it steaming hot."

"Okay." She pushed the plunger down, and then poured out two cups of coffee. "Black, that's how you have it isn't it?"

"That's right."

She handed him a cup and he took a sip while she enjoyed the aroma of her coffee. "Ah, I can even smell the difference before I taste it, and I know it'll be that much nicer."

"*Jah,* it's much better."

She sat down. "Good." She didn't feel like coffee but

she had some just to try it. "It is nice. Now, apart from going out on Saturday, I have invited Elizabeth, the girls, and William for dinner one night soon. Will you join us?"

He shook his head. "I don't think that would be a good idea. Remember, I'm the one that you dumped to take up with William."

"Oh, yes. I didn't think that through properly. *Nee*, it probably wouldn't be a good idea."

"I sincerely hope that everything goes well for you."

"For the first time in my life, I feel good about this. I always liked William and I'm so excited. I can hardly believe it," Deborah said. He smiled and took another sip of coffee. Then she felt awful for talking about how happy she was when he was feeling so low. "Is there anything I can do to help you?"

"You are helping me. Your friendship is something I value. My next step is looming. I just have to decide whether I'm staying here or going back to Sandy Creek."

"Going back for good?" She placed her coffee down on the table. The other day, he'd mentioned he'd go back for Becky's wedding.

"You don't think that's a good idea?"

"I don't. How would you feel being around Becky? There will be the wedding and then she'll be married and all that."

"*Jah*, but I can't avoid her in my life. I mean, she's made her choice, and she's happy. Isn't that what we hope will happen for those we love, that they are happy?"

"I guess that's true." She wanted to say something to cheer him up but she couldn't think of a single thing apart from what she'd already said. "I'll find out what I can from

May regarding what single ladies might be coming to her wedding."

"That's not necessary. I don't want you to make me sound desperate."

"She won't know it's for you."

He shook his head. "It'll be pretty obvious. Anyway, I'll see who I get along with on the day."

"Okay. Will you stay for dinner?"

"*Nee*, I'll drink this and I'll go. *Mamm's* better and she's got people coming for dinner. I hope she's not trying to match-make for me tonight."

"She wouldn't, would she?"

He laughed and shook his head. "I don't think so. Well, maybe."

Andrew didn't stay much longer before he left for his parents' home.

CHAPTER 17

DEBORAH HAD to wait until Friday after school to see William again. As soon as the girls jumped in the buggy, he turned to Deborah. "I'm sorry to leave things so long before seeing you again. I've had other demands on my time. Is it still okay with you to spend tomorrow with me?"

"*Jah*, it is."

"I've been looking forward to it." He glanced over his shoulder at the girls.

"Me too."

When he turned back, he asked, "Is there anything in particular you'd like to do?"

She looked into his eyes. "Not really."

"Maybe we could go for a drive and then have a picnic?"

"I'd like that." That was what she'd been thinking about the entire time. "That's exactly what I was thinking of, a picnic."

113

"I'll bring the food for us."

"Nee you can't."

"It's all arranged. Elizabeth said she'd help me with it."

"Are you sure?"

"I'm quite sure. She loves doing things like that."

"How about I bring some dessert?"

He chuckled. "I can't say no to that."

"Good."

When the girls got a little too loud, he said, "I'd better get these girls home."

"Oh, and how is Thursday next week for dinner? That's the day after May's wedding."

"Okay, that'll be fine. I'll see you tomorrow then. How does ten o'clock sound?"

"That would be perfect."

He gave her a beaming smile before he jumped into the buggy. When he drove away, Deborah turned her attention to the couple of children that were still waiting to be collected.

∾

ON SATURDAY MORNING, Deborah woke to the sun streaming in her window. It was a new day. A glorious new day.

It was only six minutes past seven, so she jumped out of bed and turned on the bath, looking forward to a leisurely soak in the tub.

While she soaked in the hot water, she was certain she heard a horse. She stayed still, and then there was no sound and no knock on her door. A few seconds later, she heard the horse again, and then nothing. It was odd that the early visitor hadn't knocked. Then she decided that the person might have thought she was still asleep since she still had all the downstairs curtains drawn.

Once she was out of the bath and dressed, she flung aside the curtains of the living room, and then she opened her door and looked out. Her gaze was drawn to a white envelope sitting on the mat in front of her on the porch. Whoever it had been, they'd left her a note. She leaned down, picked it up and turned it over. There was nothing written on either side. Holding it up to the morning sun she saw a note inside. She ripped open the envelope and pulled out a letter. Immediately, she saw it was from William.

Fearing bad news, a pain of sadness stabbed at her heart. She sank to her knees and read the letter right there in the doorway.

DEAR DEBORAH,

I've learned some disturbing news and I can't talk to you at this time. We will not be coming to your house for dinner this week. Disregard everything I said about a future with you. I cannot believe the behavior you've entered into. I will talk to you soon, but I can't say I'm not disappointed in you. I will not call for you today. Our picnic will not take place.

Sincerely,

William

THE LETTER SLIPPED from her trembling fingers. He'd

found out he'd been tricked. This is what she'd feared. He was a no-nonsense man and would see what she'd done with Andrew as deceiving him.

Instantly, the pain in her heart was replaced with a nauseous tummy. She ran out into the garden and was sick.

DEBORAH PICKED herself up off the ground and dusted down her dress. "Did you really think he'd marry you?" she said out loud. If only she'd never dared to test him, then she wouldn't have faced this disappointment.

With strong determination, she forced herself to make a simple breakfast of cereal and coffee. All the while she kept telling herself she'd lost nothing because she'd never had him in the first place. After breakfast, she kept her mind off William by writing letters to distant relatives.

When she heard a buggy, she abandoned the letters on the kitchen table and ran to the window hoping it was William with a change of heart. It was Andrew, but she wasn't disappointed. Needing a friend she ran out to meet him.

CHAPTER 18

"What is it?" Andrew asked.

She shook her head. "It's not good. I've got so much to tell you." She swallowed hard. "Come and have coffee." She made him coffee while he sat and listened to what had happened.

"Where's the letter?" he demanded.

"Just there." She nodded her head to the table, and he picked it up and read it.

Andrew tossed the letter down onto the table. "He doesn't deserve you, that's all I can say, Deborah. If he can't see what a good woman you are, he doesn't deserve you. Who does he think he is? 'We'll talk about this soon,' he says as though he has some authority over you."

"It's not that, it's just that he's very strict and straight-forward about things. Someone who strictly follows the rules, if you know what I mean."

"*Jah*, I know the type. Well, forget him. That's what I say."

"I know. I have to. It just won't be easy." She couldn't believe she'd had her hopes up so high and now she was so low.

He laughed. "We're a fine pair you and I."

"Love's not an easy road. I'm not looking forward to seeing him at May's wedding. I'm guessing that's the next time I'll see him. Or, maybe after *schul* next week. Unless Elizabeth collects the girls." She put a hand to her head. *"Ach nee.* What if he's told Elizabeth? I'm so embarrassed. She'll think I'm dreadful."

"Look, he might change his mind and see how silly he's been."

Deborah shook her head. "I doubt that will happen."

"I'll drive you to the wedding."

Deborah laughed. "We tried making him jealous, remember? That didn't work out."

"Come with me anyway?"

She looked into his hopeful face. It would be nice to have him by her side giving her strength. "Okay."

DEBORAH HAD BEEN RIGHT. Elizabeth collected the girls on both Monday and Tuesday. Because of all the community members going to May's wedding on Wednesday, school was only a half day—finishing at twelve—and many of the children didn't show up at all. Two of those absent children were Grace and Ivy.

Since receiving that horrible letter from William, Deborah had a good long think about what she wanted in a man. Her heart still wanted William, but her head told her she needed a loving and gentle man like Andrew.

Andrew was waiting for Deborah when she got home from school. While she changed into a nicer dress, he unhitched her buggy for her.

As he drove them to May's wedding, she decided to open her mind to the possibility of Andrew being the man God wanted her to marry. They both had unhappy pasts in regard to relationships and maybe that was because they were meant to find love with each other.

When they drove closer to May's parents' house, Andrew said, "There's a huge crowd here already."

"Oh dear, I told May I'd be here early. What's the time?"

He looked down at the clock in his buggy. "It's only two. Isn't the wedding starting at three?"

"That's right. These might be all of May's relatives who've come from a distance. Oh, and May's twin, April, will be here too."

"Why wouldn't she be?"

"Oh, you don't know. She married someone and moved to his community. She's having a *boppli* now, in a few months I mean, not right now." Nervousness at seeing William again was causing her to fall over her words.

He laughed. "I knew what you meant. Many things have changed since I've been gone. May and April were tiny girls and now they're all grown up."

"That's what happens. We all grow older."

They both got out of the buggy.

"It's true, it happens to the best of us—except for you. You look even prettier now than you ever did."

She laughed at the compliment, and then when she was about to respond, she noticed he had frozen in place.

He was looking over at the crowd of people as though he had seen a ghost.

"Are you okay?" she asked.

"It's Becky," he hissed. "She's here."

"Your Becky?"

Slowly, he nodded.

Deborah followed his gaze and immediately she picked out which one was Becky. She was a very pretty girl. Deborah turned back to Andrew. "Find out why she's here."

He rubbed the back of his neck, and then he said, "She's walking over."

"I hope it's good news. I must go see May. She's expecting me." She hurried off, giving Becky a smile as she passed her. Becky gave her a nod. Becky must've seen the two of them arriving together. From the look on Becky's face, Deborah knew Becky had come there for Andrew. That meant Andrew was no longer a marriage prospect for her. Today, she would put her own needs and wants aside and concentrate on her friend, May. It was her day, maybe the biggest day in her life.

People were continuously moving in and out of May's parents' house when Deborah walked through the door. She sidestepped around the men who were arranging the church benches in the living room, and then she heard giggling and followed the sound up the stairs and into May's room.

May was sitting down on the bed touching April's rounded stomach through her dress. May jumped up. "Here you are." She wrapped her arms around Deborah's neck and hugged her. "How's school?"

"The children are missing you and want you to come back as soon as possible."

"I will."

Deborah and April exchanged a hug. "You're looking so well, April, and getting so big."

April immediately started talking about being married and having a baby, and Deborah disregarded the pangs of jealousy she felt. April and May were more than ten years younger than she and they already had what Deborah wanted. Failure was all that she felt. Why had no man found her irresistible? It couldn't have been only her plain appearance keeping them away. Many plain women were married.

Once April paused for a breath, Deborah sat on the bed beside May. "You look so lovely, May, and I'm so happy for you."

"You're a good friend, Deborah. You've always been so nice to me, even when I've been …"

"Horrible?" April suggested.

"Oh, *nee,* she's never been anything like that." Deborah smiled and shook her head.

May giggled. "You've always seen the good in me, Deborah, and not everyone in my life has done that."

"When I look at you, all I see is good."

May put her arms out and gave Deborah another hug.

"You must need glasses then," April said, which made Deborah and May laugh.

"See what I mean?" May asked.

April pouted at her twin. "Don't think marriage is going to solve all your problems, May, because it won't. Some days you'll love Jeff and some days you'll hate him."

Deborah saw May's face. "Oh, April, this is May's wedding day."

"I'm just telling her things that I wish people would've told me, that's all. Anyway, you see the good in her, why can't you see the good in me?" April turned abruptly and walked out of the room.

Deborah raised her hand to her mouth. "Oh no, I didn't mean to upset her."

"Don't worry. Everything is upsetting her lately."

Deborah said, "I feel awful, but I didn't want her to say things like that on your special day."

May nodded. "I know, but in her own twisted way she was trying to be helpful."

At that moment, Abigail came into the room with her daughter, Ferris. Abigail was one of the attendants and her dress was the same dark blue as May's.

Deborah greeted them, and then she left so May could talk with Abigail while she went to find April to apologize.

She saw April in the kitchen laughing with Rebecca, the bishop's daughter. Realizing April had already forgotten what she said, she went to see if she could find out what was going on with Andrew and Becky. She walked outside to where most of the people had gathered and came face-to-face with William, who seemed shocked to see her. The feeling was mutual. He ran a hand through his hair.

"Hello, William. What's wrong? You don't look very happy."

"I'm not happy. Did you get my letter?"

"I did."

"I'm disappointed with you and with your friend."

"Which friend are you talking about?"

"Andrew. He led everybody to believe he had a broken relationship and fooled everybody into thinking that you and he had something together."

"I can't speak for my friend. But he didn't know that Becky was going to be here."

He shook his head. "I said I would talk to you, but I don't think this is either the time or the place."

Sudden anger rose within her. "I have nothing to say to you and I don't need to listen to any of your reprimands or judgemental accusations. I'm not a child, William."

"I would rather we talked it over than you being cross with me."

She folded her arms across her chest. "There's really nothing to say. Anyway, when did you think I was fooling you?"

"Don't try to do it again." He shook a finger at her. "Elizabeth heard it from someone who overheard it from Aunt Agatha's own lips."

Deborah wondered exactly what he had heard. "So, you've got third hand information, or was it fourth?"

He drew his eyebrows together.

She continued, "We can talk about it tomorrow after school if you think there's anything at all to discuss."

"*Jah,* I do. Tomorrow will be fine." He turned and walked away.

She knew he felt tricked, but that hadn't been her intention. *I should've just listened to myself.* Looking around, she caught sight of Becky and Andrew talking in a far corner of the yard. They were back together. She could see it in his eyes even from a distance.

Throughout the wedding, Deborah sat with Rebecca and Karen, who was expecting her second set of twins any day. It wasn't easy for Deborah being surrounded by married women many of whom were pregnant. The close relationship she had with her students was some compensation for her being childless. Hopefully, when her students grew up, they would look back fondly on their schooldays and remember her.

CHAPTER 19

DEBORAH FOUND Aunt Agatha in the kitchen after most of the guests had been served. "Can I have a word with you?"

Aunt Agatha swung around. *"Jah."*

Deborah stepped forward. "In private."

When they left the kitchen, Deborah found a quiet spot in the living room where they both sat down. All the wedding guests were outside eating at the tables under the annexes. "Somehow, William found out and now everything between us is finished. We were going out somewhere on Saturday and he just left me alone for the whole day. I woke up to a note on my doormat telling we were through."

"How did he find out?"

"He said Elizabeth overheard it. Or someone over-heard, and then told Elizabeth."

"This is terrible. It's my fault. I shouldn't have told anyone. I was pleased for you."

Deborah sighed. "It doesn't matter."

"I'm sorry, but he should be flattered you took so much trouble to make him notice you."

"I doubt he'll see things like that."

"He should."

"I just don't know what to do about it. I thought you should know since you were so good in helping me."

Aunt Agatha patted her on her shoulder. "I wouldn't have told you to do that if I knew it was going to—"

"It doesn't matter. What's done is done."

"I'll find someone else for you and what better time than right now?" Aunt Agatha's wicked grin returned.

Deborah shook her head. "Please don't. I need to recover from this first." Deborah stood up and Aunt Agatha reached up her hand to be pulled out of the soft couch.

When she stood, Agatha said, "Go and enjoy the rest of the wedding."

"Okay. I'll try."

BECAUSE ANDREW WAS SO WRAPPED up with talking to Becky, they were among the last guests to leave the wedding.

Deborah had been helping in the kitchen while she waited. When she saw Becky leave with some people, she didn't waste any time joining Andrew. "What happened?" she asked.

"I'll tell you everything soon. Are you ready to go?"

"I've been ready for the last two hours."

He grimaced. "Sorry."

"Let's go." She strode toward the buggy.

126

"It was a lovely wedding," Andrew said, as they both climbed into the buggy.

"Jah, May's very happy," She did her best to fix a smile on her face.

"What's wrong?"

"I'm fine."

"Nee, you're not. I can see you've been crying." He steered the horse and buggy onto the road.

"I might as well tell you. Things between William and me are over ... over before they even had a chance to begin."

"You talked with him?"

She nodded, unable to speak.

"What happened?"

Deborah took a deep breath. "He said he wanted to talk and I said there's nothing to say. He insisted. Then we decided to talk tomorrow."

"Is that all?"

She nodded.

"That doesn't sound so bad."

"You read the letter. It was awful. He was so unkind and I could feel he was hostile toward me. It was a stupid idea and I shouldn't have listened to Agatha."

"She's wise. One of the wisest women in the community."

"I know. I shouldn't have been rude about her. I just feel so wretched. A couple of days ago I thought everything was turning out right and now it's all come crashing down about my ears." When he was silent, she asked, "What happened with you and Becky?"

A smile fixed upon his face. "She's no longer getting married."

"She's not?"

"Nee. She said she loves me and she missed me and that's why she came to find me."

"What does that mean?"

"That means I'm going back with her."

Deborah could hardly believe it. He was going back to the same woman who'd dumped him. "You're what?"

"Going back home with her."

Now she was losing him as a friend, again, at the very worst time. "Oh, this is so unexpected." She rubbed her forehead shielding her face from him, so he wouldn't see how disappointed she was.

"But you are happy for me, right?"

"I'm happy for you, if that's what you've decided and you're sure, but I'm miserable for myself. See what kind of person I am? I'm awful. He's right about me. I'm a terrible person."

"You have to stop saying that or you'll start believing it."

She kept quiet. Then, when they were almost at her home, she spoke again. "At least one of us will have love in their lives. All the friends we've grown up with are married. It was just us two left."

"You'll find someone too. You've just got to believe it."

She nodded, remembering. Only a day or two ago she had been telling him the exact same thing.

CHAPTER 20

AFTER THE DISASTROUS happenings at May's wedding, Deborah still faced the awful conversation that she knew she was going to have with William after school. She could feel it looming over her head all day Thursday, just like the storm clouds in the sky, as she did her best to focus on her students.

When school was over, she walked with Ivy and Grace to William's waiting buggy. He jumped down and with a stern face, told the girls to get into the buggy while he had a word with Miss Deborah.

She figured the straightforward approach was best. She made sure the girls were in the back of the buggy before she spoke. "What have I done that was so awful?" All was lost between them, she knew that, but she deserved respect.

"There is one thing I detest above all else, and that's a scheming woman. You had me believe there was something happening between you and your friend, Andrew …"

"You've—"

He cut her off not giving her a chance to speak. "There's no point adding to my disappointment by denying it. I have it straight from Aunt Agatha's mouth."

"She would not have said that to you. Who told you that? What you heard was third or fourth hand, wasn't it? There's a name for when people hear things that are repeated and then repeated again, but I can't quite remember it."

He shook his head, his expression showing how disgusted he was in her. "From someone who heard it from her lips. You can imagine how disappointed I was."

"I'm sorry I have disappointed you."

"Deborah, you should not be sorry that you disappointed me. You should be sorry for what you've done."

She felt like a child and disliked having his disapproval. Deep in her heart, she had thought it wrong at the time, but she was desperate for him to love her. "Do you think you could forgive me?"

"I can forgive you. I can, *jah.* But, what I said about marriage the other day no longer applies and then, with that being said, we can no longer spend time together."

She looked over at the girls hoping they couldn't hear anything or see the way he was talking to her.

He followed her gaze, and then said, "The girls are my problem. Don't concern yourself with them other than being their teacher."

Tears formed in her eyes. If only she hadn't built everything up in her mind to think she was going to be the stepmother to Ivy and Grace. "I'm sorry it all happened."

"As am I."

She had to walk away before he saw she was holding back tears.

"Bye, Miss Deborah."

She swallowed hard and turned around with a smile. "Bye, girls."

William didn't even say goodbye as she walked back to the schoolhouse. By then, all of the other children had been collected, so she locked the schoolhouse, walked around the building and got into her buggy. During school hours, she always kept her horse and buggy behind the schoolhouse, so she couldn't see William driving away, but she heard his buggy.

She sat there as the tears flowed down her cheeks. She was a person who always tried to do the right thing by everybody and now she felt like a naughty child.

She dried her eyes as best she could and headed home just as the rain came. She shook her head and looked up at the gray sky. "Why can't I just find a man who loves me without me having to struggle to have him notice me?" And then a picture of Andrew came into her mind. Perhaps the man for her was Andrew, but if that was so, why had Becky come to find him? She needed to talk to somebody and have them tell her everything would be alright. At times like these she missed her parents. They had always been on her side. Then there was Andrew, who was so good at calming her down and helping her think positively.

She took a detour and found herself heading past

Andrew's family home. Even though she wanted to talk to him, she didn't want to talk to his parents or his family. It was no use, he was nowhere in sight. Through the light rain and the dark clouds that blocked the afternoon sun, she steered her horse toward home. When her house came into view, her heart filled with gladness—there was Andrew's buggy.

With the rain still falling, she moved her horse into the undercover section of the barn and Andrew hurried over to her.

As soon as he saw her, he said, "You're upset."

"Well, I had a talk with him today, just now, that's why."

His lips turned downward and he shook his head. "I take it things didn't go well?"

"Really bad."

"You make me a cup of hot tea and after I unhitch the buggy for you I'll make us a nice fire."

She blew out a deep breath, ever so thankful for her good friend, and got out of the buggy. "Okay, that sounds good, thanks."

As she walked to the house, he yelled out, "Make sure you change out of those wet clothes."

Deborah hadn't even noticed she was walking through the rain without a coat. "I will." As soon as she got inside, she placed the teakettle on the stove and then hurried to change her damp dress for a dry one. Normally, she would've just made a fire and let it dry by itself, but she'd gotten a heavy scolding from one man today and didn't want to get into trouble with another.

What was she going to do when Andrew went back to

Sandy Creek? In the short time he'd been back home she'd come to rely on his friendship. She didn't know what she was going to do when he left. When she found the coffee he liked, she remembered he'd asked for a hot tea.

"I have your hot tea ready," she called out from the kitchen when she heard him walk in the door.

"I'll light that fire first. Then we can sit in front of it while we drink our tea."

"That sounds good." She brought out the tea and some cookies on a tray and set it down on the table in front of the couch. In no time, they sat in front of a crackling fire. "Tell me about Becky. How did it happen that you—"

"I know in my heart things will work out for you."

"That's what everyone says. Just tell me about you and Becky. I'm sick of myself and thinking about all my worries. I just want some good news."

He chuckled. "There's not much to it, really. She missed me and she's told the other man she can't marry him because she's in love with me."

Deborah didn't know why Becky had left him in the first place, but didn't like to ask. She thought back to Andrew saying how Becky had pointed out his faults to him back when she'd broken off their relationship.

"That's wonderful," she said after a pause, "and I suppose you'll be getting married?"

He raised his eyebrows. "Under the circumstances, we'll probably have to wait a while since she's just disappointed the other man. We have to be considerate of his feelings. I know how hard I took it."

"*Jah,* that would be a difficult situation."

"Our bishop in Sandy Creek is strict, which never helps such matters."

She couldn't stop the tears that suddenly fell down her cheeks. She set her teacup down on the table and wiped her eyes. "I'm sorry. I've been holding it all in ever since I talked with William. It was just so awful." All she wanted was to have somebody in her life. A man to share her life with, somebody to appreciate her when she cleaned the house nicely, or made a special dinner. Every other woman in the community had that without having to worry and strive for it. What was wrong with her?

"Please don't cry." He put his arm around her shoulders.

She looked into his eyes wondering if he was in love with Becky or whether he was just going along with the flow of things because she had come back to him. If Becky hadn't appeared out of nowhere, could Andrew and she have become more than friends? "Do you truly love Becky?"

"I do." He stared at her. "Why do you ask?"

"I thought there might be … I thought at one stage … I wondered if ..."

He chuckled. "I wondered about that too, but I think it's because we were both lonely and we were there when we needed each other."

But I still need you, she screamed in her head. But he had made his choice clear. "Where's Becky now?"

"She's staying with a cousin of hers, Veronica."

"Oh. I didn't realize she was Veronica's cousin."

"I think most probably a second cousin, or maybe a third cousin of Veronica's."

Deborah nodded. *"Jah,* that might be."

"Cheer up. You must come to my wedding, all right?"

She laughed. "In Sandy Creek?"

"Jah."

"I might do that. It's been so good having you back here. You're such a good friend and I don't want to lose you. I'm happy for you that Becky realized it was you she loved."

"Don't get me wrong, I'm mad at her. I have to pray, and check my anger, because I'm still furious with her for putting me through everything."

Deborah was taken aback. She'd never heard him express anger or disapproval of any kind. "Oh, I didn't realize."

"It's true, but I have to find a way to forgive her. I can't let that stand in the way of the love I have for her."

Deborah looked into the orange flickers of the fire as the hues changed from yellow, through to orange and then red. If Andrew could forgive the woman he loved, would William be able to forgive her? Could she also forgive William?

CHAPTER 21

ANDREW TOOK his arm away from Deborah's shoulders and picked up his teacup. "What are you thinking about?"

"Just how I disappointed him. He kept using that word over and over again. That was what was in his heart. He can never forgive me for the deception."

"Just give him time. Sometimes all people need is a chance to see things clearly. One thing I've learned is feelings don't go away. Once you've had strong love for someone that feeling's always there no matter how they disappoint you."

Deborah picked up her teacup and warmed her hands around it. "At least you introduced me to good *kaffe*."

"Somebody had to."

She giggled. *"Jah,* my *kaffe* was pretty dreadful."

"I'm heading back home on Friday week. Not this coming Friday, the one after."

"So soon?"

He nodded. "And I should say, we'll be heading back on Friday."

"Why don't you bring Becky over for dinner tomorrow night?"

He dipped his head and stared at her. "You certain you'd be up to it?"

She giggled making light of how she truly felt. "I'm used to disappointment. I'm able to bounce back quickly."

"Tomorrow will be just fine. We've got every other night booked up at different people's houses."

"Perfect. Having the both of you to cook for will keep my mind off William and I'm looking forward to getting to know Becky."

"What you need is to get yourself a dog."

"A dog?"

"That's right. For company."

She wriggled uncomfortably. "But I go to school every day and it would be left alone. *Nee.*"

He shrugged his shoulders. "I suppose. I'm going to miss you. We'll both be married soon enough."

She rolled her eyes.

"Don't give up on him."

"I have given up on William. I'm not going to wait around for the rest of my life for him to change his mind."

"You might not have to. Just give it a few months. Keep away from him and then just see what happens. He'll come around."

"Do you think so?" She was just being polite because she had no intention of getting her hopes up again.

"I do. Becky came back to me."

"Things are vastly different in the two relationships.

You didn't do anything silly. I concocted a plan to force him to like me."

"You can't force anybody to like you, and you did nothing wrong. All we did was spend some time together which we probably would've done anyway."

Deborah sighed. *"Jah,* but the intention was to deceive by spending so much time together on that Saturday and Sunday."

"Do you regret it?"

She shook her head. "Regret's a pointless thing. I did what I did and now I'll just live with whatever comes next."

"And what's the worst thing that can happen?" he asked.

"I live the rest of my life alone. That's not so bad, and maybe one day I will get a dog, or even a cat. Maybe two or three cats like Aunt Agatha. She seems happy enough."

"Speaking of Aunt Agatha, I hear she might have a male friend."

"What?" Deborah laughed thinking he was joking.

"It's true."

Deborah held her stomach and laughed. "Like a boyfriend? A man who's a friend but more than a friend?"

"Exactly."

"Nee. I doubt it. She's ancient and I'm sure she wouldn't be interested anymore."

He took a sip of his tea. "That's what I heard. How old do you think she would be?"

"One hundred?" She giggled, unable to imagine Aunt Agatha courting at her age.

His eyes twinkled with amusement. "That's not nice. She could be anything between seventy and ninety."

"How old is the male friend of hers and how did you find out about them?"

"I heard a few things from someone. I can't say who."

"How's that possible? I would've heard it before you."

"Perhaps it's just a rumor and there's no truth in it."

"I think you're right about that. There's no one in this community and she hasn't visited anywhere."

"I must have heard wrong then."

Another thought occurred to Deborah. "It would be funny if Aunt Agatha married before me."

"To do that she would have to have a man hiding somewhere."

Deborah rubbed her neck. "And so would I." He opened his mouth to speak and she cut across him. "I know I know, give him some time." In her heart, Deborah knew she couldn't give him any time. What she needed was a man who was also her best friend. Was she allowing the man whom she was meant to be with to walk out of her life without making any effort to stop him?

"I should give you some peace and quiet. I'm sure you've got to get the dinner prepared for tomorrow."

"Tomorrow? What's happening tomorrow?" she joked.

"How quickly you forget me."

She laughed. "I won't forget you're coming to dinner. It'll only be something simple. Don't expect a grand feast or anything."

"Anything is fine with me and it will be for Becky too."

"Oh yes. I do have certain things I have to prepare for tomorrow's lessons. I have to prepare assessments."

Schoolwork was the last thing she felt like doing, as was entertaining the very woman who was about to take away her best friend.

"What time should we arrive?"

"Between six and six thirty."

"I think we can work with that."

"Good. I'll see you then."

He jumped to his feet and she walked him out.

As soon as he left, she threw herself against the closed door. Inviting Becky and Andrew to dinner the next tonight was possibly the worst thing she could have done. Forcing herself away from the door, she headed over to collect the tea items from the coffee table.

Carrying them into the kitchen, she told herself if she was going to be miserable she might as well be miserable in a clean and tidy house. As she rinsed out the cups, her mind drifted again to William and what he thought of her. At the very least, the whole thing was embarrassing.

From William's point of view, she knew he thought she had been deliberately setting out to trap him and there was the truth. Then again, he had to have a little interest in her to have fallen prey to that trap.

After a dinner of reheated vegetables and noodle soup, she sat by the fire planning out the menu for tomorrow night's dinner. A quick trip to the markets after school tomorrow was needed.

Normally, she shopped once a week but her routine had been interrupted recently. She shook her head vigorously trying to drive William from her mind. Looking up at the clock on the mantle, she saw it was still early, so she reached for her needlework sampler to fill in the next hour before bed.

As she sewed, she saw the scar on her finger and remembered the night she went to William's place for dinner. That was the closest she'd come to finding love.

CHAPTER 22

THE NEXT DAY, Deborah wondered how William would react to her. Would he surprise her and apologize for being so harsh? After school Deborah was disappointed to see Elizabeth was the one who was there to collect the children.

"It's nice to see you again, Elizabeth."

"And you."

"William couldn't come today?"

"He's busy and he asked me to collect the children."

Deborah smiled knowing that it was too awkward for him to face her. "Well, I think they've both had a good day."

"*Jah*, we have," said Ivy.

"I've had a good day too, but I want to go home and play. Will you show us how to cook again, Aunt Elizabeth?"

"Of course I will. We'll do the dinner together again."

Grace cheered, and then Ivy gave Grace a small tug on her sleeve. "Let's get into the buggy."

BEFORE DEBORAH HEADED home to cook for Andrew and Becky, she had to stop in at the markets to collect a few items. She always bought her fruit and vegetables from the Whileys' stall, which was now May's new husband's family stall. The last thing she expected was to run into William there. With a bag of potatoes in her hand, she walked around the corner to pay for them when she came face-to-face with him.

"Oh, I'm sorry," she said, as she stepped aside.

He frowned at her and grunted and went to walk away.

She would not let him get away with that behavior toward her. It was downright rude. "Why are you acting so hostile toward me?"

"Because I can scarcely believe what you've done. I had always held you in high regard and if it'd been anybody else who had done what you did it wouldn't have mattered so much." Still frowning, he shook his head. "I find it hard to believe what happened. It just doesn't seem like something you would do and that's why I was so disappointed."

Now she knew all was lost and he would never like her again. She wanted to get some information from him about why men never found her attractive. "I just have one question for you."

"*Jah?* Go ahead."

"You told me you were interested in me, but never did anything about it."

He nodded. *"Jah,* it's true."

"Can I ask why? Is it because I'm a plain-looking woman and there are other women around more attractive?"

He drew his eyebrows together. "Why are you putting it down to looks? Things like that aren't important to me."

She pressed her lips together knowing she was never going to get a proper answer out of him. A shade above ugly was how she saw herself and she knew that was how others saw her as well. That was what the real problem was; he just didn't want to admit it. Calling his bluff, she said, "Won't you forgive me, so we can move past this and get back to where we were?"

He shook his head. "I can forgive you, but you don't have the qualities I need in a *fraa.* It's not just me I have to think about, it's my girls as well. If I'm going to bring a woman into their lives it must be someone with high values and outstandingly good behavior."

She couldn't argue with him about that. She'd embarrassed herself enough for one day.

"It's not about how you look," he added, which only make her feel worse. She picked up her bag of potatoes and turned away to pay for her purchase. Neither of them said goodbye.

On Deborah's way home, she decided she would put all her energy into making a nice dinner for Andrew and Becky.

~

As Deborah sat across from Andrew and Becky she noticed how Andrew looked at Becky. He'd never looked at her that way, but William had—once. She'd had a fleeting chance to see what true love was like and maybe that was all she would get. What if God wanted her to remain single all her life so she could continue to teach other people's children? It was an important job and she told herself to be satisfied with everything *Gott* had given. This life was just a vapor, which would quickly fade, so what did it matter if she didn't find love? She was *Gott's* servant and not the other way around. Her prayers had gone unanswered, but *Gott* wasn't her servant to grant all of her wishes like some genie out of a bottle. Or—maybe more accurately worded—sometimes *Gott's* answer was, "No, my child. I have a better plan."

When she saw Andrew and Becky smile at one another, a pain stabbed at her heart. Not that she begrudged their relationship, she was happy for them. If she was going to be single forever why had *Gott* given her that hunger in her heart to find love?

"This is really good," Becky said, regarding the food.

"*Denke.* It's only a simple chicken stew. I'm not much of a cook and I didn't have much time to get it prepared."

"You did an amazing job," Andrew said.

"*Denke.* Do either of you want more before dessert? There's plenty there."

"I wouldn't mind a little more chicken," Andrew said.

"And you, Becky?"

"I'm fine, *denke.*"

She piled more chicken onto his plate.

"That's more than enough." He chuckled.

Becky giggled. "Andrew does like his food."

"I've noticed."

"How long have the two of you been friends?" Becky asked.

Seeing that Andrew's mouth was full of food, Deborah answered, "For practically as long as I can remember. Probably from about the age of thirteen, wouldn't you say so, Andrew?"

Andrew nodded and swallowed his mouthful. "About that."

"I can't believe there was never any romantic involvement between the two of you."

Deborah looked at Becky, surprised, as the realization hit her. Becky must have heard that the two of them were spending time together and she'd come all this way to win him back. Deborah's plan for her and William had failed, but it had worked for Andrew in getting Becky back. "It just never occurred to us," she told Becky, who appeared relieved. "Are you both excited to be heading back on Friday?"

"We'll have a few things to sort through once we get back, but once we get over those things everything will be better."

Becky nodded at what Andrew said, knowing he was speaking of the trouble that might be caused by Becky's recent ex-fiancé being upset. She felt sorry for him, whoever he was, since she knew firsthand what it was like to be rejected.

It was hard for Deborah to keep the conversation flowing because she could sense the couple wanted to be alone. As soon as Andrew had eaten a second serving of dessert, Deborah said, "I won't be offended if you want to leave. I'm sure there are many things you've got to discuss and you probably can't do that if you're staying at different people's houses."

Andrew glanced over at Becky and she smiled. Looking back at Deborah, he said, "You really don't mind?"

"Of course I don't mind. Leave as soon as you want."

"Normally, we'd want to stay here and talk with you, but you're right, there are a lot of things we need to discuss and that will buy us some time. Thanks for understanding."

"That's what friends are for."

Becky looked across the table. "We can't leave without helping you wash all these dishes."

"There aren't that many. You two go do your planning."

"Are you sure you don't mind?"

"I'm positive." Deborah rose to her feet. "I'll walk you both out."

Andrew jumped up and Becky stayed seated. "I wouldn't feel right about—"

"Deborah said it was okay," Andrew interrupted.

"Are you certain?" Becky asked.

Deborah smiled liking Becky more every moment. *"Jah,* I don't mind. Besides, I'd never let my guests do the washing up."

"Okay, *denke.* And, the dinner was *wunderbaar."*

"You're very welcome." She walked them to the door and they stopped to put on their coats. Andrew helped Becky into her coat while Deborah looked on. As soon as

Becky had her coat on and Andrew was getting into his, Becky leaned in to give Deborah a hug.

"*Denke* for the meal and having us here tonight. It was so nice to meet you after all Andrew's told me about you."

"I'm delighted to have met you, too. I wish you great joy in life."

Becky smiled her thanks and looked over at Andrew. "Are you ready?" he asked her. It was like they were a married couple already.

"*Jah.*"

Andrew said, "We'll see you before we go."

"I hope so. Don't you dare leave without saying goodbye."

"We won't."

Deborah held the door open and, by the light of the porch lantern, watched them walk through the semidarkness to the buggy.

When the buggy was out of sight she closed the door and had a pang of envy over the many exciting plans they had to make. As she dipped the dishes in the warm sudsy water, she had a feeling that many people wouldn't approve of what Becky had done. Bishop Elmer didn't like people getting in and out of relationships quickly, and the bishop at Sandy Creek—she'd heard—was no different.

But still, that would be but a glitch for Andrew and Becky in their lifetime of happiness. To truly be happy herself, the only thing Deborah could do was resign herself to being single–to embrace being single–and stop looking around for a man who might make a suitable husband. It only led to disappointment. If *Gott* wanted her to have a husband, He'd have to work it out without her help.

She picked up a tea towel feeling much better. A weight had lifted off her shoulders. Now that she knew she wasn't going to marry, she was annoyed with William for being judgemental with her scheme to make him jealous. No one had forced him to pay her any attention. As Deborah dried the plates, she did her best to put William out of her mind once again and be pleased for the happiness Andrew and Becky shared.

CHAPTER 23

FRIDAY AFTERNOON WAS when Deborah next saw William. She took a deep breath, and was ready to lead the girls to his buggy and then they ran off ahead to meet him. "Bye, girls," she said and then quickly turned around. Then she heard his voice.

"Deborah, can I speak with you for a moment?"

Deborah swung around, startled to see how quickly he'd closed the distance between them. *"Jah?"* Her heart pounded. She hoped he wasn't going to say he was pulling the girls out of school. Something like that would look really bad with the school board. She should never have gotten involved with one of the parents.

He gave a quick look over his shoulder at the girls, who were climbing into the buggy, his expression serious but not stern, and then he turned to Deborah. "Can we talk?"

"Sure. Is anything wrong?"

"May I stop by your *haus* this afternoon after I take the girls home?"

She frowned. "If it's something to do with the girls, I'm here by seven thirty every morning, and I'm willing to stay later in the afternoon if that's easier for you."

He shook his head. "It's not about the girls. It's about you and me."

"You've said what you had to say. If you've left something unsaid then let it remain unsaid. I don't wish to have any more disappointments in my life. I only want to be happy and do my work and keep to myself."

"Please, Deborah? It will only take a couple of moments."

"Okay." She sighed in resignation. "Shall we say five o'clock?"

He gave a quick nod. "*Jah.* I can make it at five."

She turned away from him and walked back to the schoolhouse. There was one young girl, Sally, still waiting for her mother to collect her. "Your *mudder* isn't usually late."

Sally nodded solemnly. Then she looked up the road and pointed. "Look! Here she is."

In the doorway of the one room schoolhouse, Deborah waited until Sally was safely in the buggy with her mother. When Deborah had waved goodbye to them, she heaved a sigh. There were so many things people took for granted, like getting married and having children. Deborah was sure that if she were ever married she'd thank God every waking moment, and even more so if she'd been blessed with children, but none of that was ever going to happen.

After she had carried her box of books to the buggy, she walked back and locked the door. She'd taken the children's writing books home to look over so she could more easily see how each child was progressing. Just because she had been a little distracted of late didn't mean that the children's education had to suffer. And May's absence because of her visiting tour after her wedding was not helping matters. May's constant chatter whenever they had free moments had become something she looked forward to every bit as much as the help with the students.

~

DEBORAH WAS STILL CROSS with William and didn't want to allow him inside. She deliberately chose not to boil the kettle just before he arrived because he had said he'd only take five minutes of her time, and that was all she would spare him.

She heard the rattling of the buggy five minutes before he was due to arrive. She threw on her shawl against the cold and stepped out onto the porch. While he was securing his horse, she sat down on one of the porch chairs. It was a chilly afternoon and it would've been much nicer to sit in front of the toasty fire, but she'd warm herself by eating dinner by the fire after he left.

Just before William reached the steps to her *haus,* he tipped his hat back slightly. "Hello, Deborah."

"Hello, William. I thought you'd be more comfortable out here on the porch."

"The porch is fine. May I sit?"

"Jah."

Once he was seated in the chair closest to the stairs, he cleared his throat. "I've come to apologize to you."

"What for?"

"For the way I treated you, and the terrible things I said."

She was relieved it was nothing to do with the girls or her as their teacher. "You were just saying what was in your mind and in your heart. It hurt me at the time, but I respect what you had to say. It means a lot that you've apologized, and I choose to forgive you. We have to see each other nearly every day because of me being the community's teacher, so I'm glad we've cleared the air." She fixed a smile on her face, determined not to let him see how much he'd upset her.

"I was hoping you would be able to fully forgive me ... and, um, that things might go back to how they were before? Could we wind back the clock?"

"For the purposes of what?"

"I was hoping that you and I ..."

Shaking her head, she said, "I don't know if we're suited."

"I think we are. Very much so."

She stared at him. Had someone talked with him? "Why the sudden change?"

He inhaled deeply. "I was scared. Scared of things moving too quickly."

Deborah slowly shook her head once again, not quite convinced by his explanation. "I don't know. From what you said, it sounded like you were casting judgement on me and what I'd done. Mind you, I'm not proud of it and I would never do anything like that again. But I hope you realize how badly hurt I was by what you said and how you talked to me."

"I do know that, and that's part of my apology. In my fear, I lashed out at you, and I shouldn't have." He looked down, shook his head regretfully and then lifted his eyes to hers. "You asked me a question the other day and I didn't answer it properly. I noticed you, Deborah, I did, but I never thought you'd be interested in a widower like me. I convinced myself you'd be suited to a different kind of man, a man far better than I. When I saw you with that friend of yours, though, it made me realize that maybe you and I could have something together."

She looked at him curiously, trying to work out what he was saying. Did he think that Andrew wasn't a worthy kind of a man? "Do you think there's something wrong with Andrew?"

He laughed. "Not at all. It's hard to explain, but I had a different man in mind for you."

She didn't feel ready to forgive him. She still wanted to be mad with him. "I'm still not sure what you mean."

"What I mean is, I'm truly sorry. I was rude to you when you said sorry to me the other day. Now I'm apologizing to you. I hope you can forgive me."

"Of course I will, and do."

He smiled as a relieved expression altered his face. "Is there is any chance for us?"

"To …?"

"To go back to where we were headed before I acted like such a fool."

She was surprised to hear him change his mind so

quickly, and felt it was too late. Now, after all that had gone on, she believed she needed someone softer than William. Tough on the outside, but gentle on the inside. "I don't know, William. What happened between the two of us really upset me." She paused, wanting to use exactly the right words and she didn't want to give him false hope when she knew there was none. "We're not suited. If we were well-matched we wouldn't even be having this conversation."

"I don't agree—I guess I'm coming at it from a different perspective. When two people are getting to know one another, there are always adjustments that need to be made. We know each other from seeing each other almost every day, but we don't know each other's likes and dislikes, wants and needs. You only learn about those things by being close with somebody. I want to be close like that with you, Deborah." His voice was much softer now.

She nearly relented, but there was too much hurt inside. If she said yes everything in their relationship would always be his way and in his timing. Now she realized it was respect she wanted from him and not only his love.

"What are you thinking about?" he asked. "Please talk to me."

"Just the whole thing. Everything that's happened. I can't just let it go. I came around to talk with you and you wouldn't listen. You shut me down and pushed me away. Now, when you feel like everything's okay you want to just wind back the clock. Words cannot be unsaid."

He bounded to his feet. "Okay. I've said what I came to

say and if you won't forgive me then there's nothing I can do about that. You and I were just never meant to be." He turned away and stomped down her porch steps.

She was shocked at his abruptness, and then she knew she had done the right thing. Jumping to her feet, she leaned over the railing. "The truth is, William Bronstein ..."

He stopped in his tracks, turned around, and glared at her.

"You're too rude and judgemental for me." She crossed her arms over her chest and stood with her feet firmly planted.

Without saying a word, he untied the horse, jumped up into the buggy, and then drove away.

She bit her lip hoping she'd done the right thing. Anger had gotten the better of her, but she'd spoken the truth of what had been on her heart. He deserved to hear the truth and she felt better to let it out.

CHAPTER 24

Wanting to confide in someone, Deborah found Aunt Agatha after the next Sunday meeting.

"I heard what happened, and I'm so sorry that he overheard it from my lips."

"I never should've done it in the first place. The whole thing was my fault. Some men might even think it funny, some would be flattered, but a man like William..." She shook her head. "And I knew that about him."

"Will you come for dinner tomorrow night and we'll talk about things? I'll make a nice pot roast and apple pie."

"*Denke.* I'll look forward to that. I don't have many people to talk with about things of a personal nature. It would be different if I had a *schweschder.* Or if I still had my *mudder.*" All the women her age were married and busy with their children.

"You have a lot of friends, don't you?"

"I do, but I don't want to burden anyone with my problems."

"What about May?"

"We have become good friends, but she's so much younger and I feel she should be taking advice from me, not the other way around."

"I know what you mean."

"Anyway, May will be away through another week and a half at least. What time would you like me to arrive tomorrow?"

"Six o'clock."

"Denke, I'll look forward to it." She glanced over and saw William's sister. It had been announced at the meeting that she would be leaving on Wednesday. "I'll just hurry over and say goodbye to Elizabeth while William's not around."

"All right, Deborah. I'll see you tomorrow night."

"I'll bring dessert. Don't make the apple pie. I'll bring something. I don't wish you to go to too much trouble."

"There's no need. You're working hard at school all day. It's no bother for me. I enjoy cooking."

"Are you sure?"

Aunt Agatha nodded. "Quite sure."

Deborah left Aunt Agatha and hurried over to Elizabeth. "Hello. I don't know if I'll be seeing you at the school this week so I wanted to say how nice it was to meet you." She sat down next to Elizabeth.

"And you too, Deborah. You know, William thinks very highly of you."

Deborah gave an embarrassed giggle. Maybe he had thought highly of her before this whole business happened. "That's good to know."

"And I'm not just talking about you being Ivy and Grace's teacher."

She peered into Elizabeth's face, knowing Elizabeth was trying to make a point about something. William had clearly said something to her. "That's a little bit of a surprise."

"I know he'll make things right with you."

"I appreciate you telling me the this and we did have a talk about it the other day." She hoped that was enough to stop Elizabeth talking of William. "I'll keep your husband in my prayers."

Elizabeth leaned over and touched Deborah lightly on her arm. "Would you?"

Deborah nodded.

"I would really appreciate that."

"I hope he'll be well enough to come here with you next time."

Elizabeth smiled brightly. "I hope so too. That would be a real miracle."

"Then we have to keep believing for a miracle. Bye now. I'm heading home." Deborah leaned over and gave Elizabeth a hug.

DEBORAH ARRIVED home from that meeting feeling as lonely as ever. Sunday was the day of rest, and no chores were permitted apart from the chores that had to be done, such as minimum meal preparation and feeding of the livestock. Without being able to throw herself into a project, Sunday afternoon was often a lonely time for Deborah.

CHAPTER 25

AFTER SHE HAD UNHITCHED the buggy and tended to her horse, she ambled over to her house thinking of things she could do to while away the time until darkness fell.

She lit the fire, and then she decided to write some long-overdue letters. She had two cousins on opposite sides of the country from one another, and whom she'd never met. Settling herself down with pen and paper she wrote a long letter to each of them. When she had addressed and sealed both envelopes, she wondered if she should take an extended holiday and visit her cousins. Each of her cousins had urged her to visit and stay as long as she wished. Maybe she should've done that many years ago, and if she had done things a little differently she might be married by now. She rubbed her head when she reminded herself that each of her friends had found love within their own community—except for Andrew.

If Andrew hadn't left all those years ago, they might have married each other. In distress, she bit her knuckle.

For her own sanity, she had to put both Andrew and William out of her mind, and stop dwelling on the fact that she would never marry.

Maybe keeping a pet, as someone had suggested, might be the right thing to do. At least then she'd have something to care for, look after, and love.

Deborah curled up on the couch and closed her eyes, and within minutes, she'd dozed off. She woke because it was cold. It was pitch black outside and the fire had gone out. She reached for the lantern beside her and flicked it. As she headed to the kitchen to heat up soup, she was pleased the lonely hours of the afternoon were behind her. Now she knew why Aunt Agatha had all those cats.

THE NEXT DAY Deborah was back in her normal routine. When the school day was over, she hoped that Ivy and Grace would be collected by one of their aunts, but that wasn't the case. Instead of walking to take the girls over to their father as she once used to, she said goodbye to them at the school door and watched them run to him. Out of the corner of her eye, saw him get out of the buggy, and get the children organized. She didn't relax until they had gone.

ON THE WAY HOME, she posted the letters to her two cousins. When she got home, she did some quick cleaning chores that she had forgotten to do over the weekend and then jumped in the waiting buggy and headed to Aunt Agatha's. On the way there, she prayed that Aunt Agatha would have some wise advice to give her ... even though her last advice had been askew.

When she got to Agatha's opened front door, she noticed two cats sitting just inside the door.

"Aunt Agatha, hello, it's Deborah. I'm here."

She appeared in front of her. "You're here already?"

"I am. It's six o'clock."

"Is it? Already?"

"Jah."

"Oh dear. Come in. You sit in the living room. I've just got a couple more things to do in the kitchen. I won't be long."

"I can help."

"Nee! You sit!"

She was taken aback by Agatha's stern voice. "Okay. I'll sit down." As soon as she sat, a black cat jumped right up on her lap. Not knowing if the cat was friendly or not, she raised her hand to pat it. When the cat purred, she decided it was safe enough to pat.

When Deborah heard a buggy outside, she didn't think much of it. But then when she heard footsteps on the porch, she hoped with everything within her that Agatha hadn't invited anyone else for dinner. She'd so been looking forward to a heart-to-heart discussion with her. And she hadn't changed from her unflattering dark green "uniform" dress after school, figuring there was no need to dress up for Aunt Agatha.

There was a knock on the door and, as it wasn't her house, she stayed seated and allowed Agatha to answer it. It was when she heard William's voice that she jumped to her feet and hurried to the front door. "Oh,

William, I didn't know you'd be here too. Are you here for dinner?"

"I invited him," Aunt Agatha said, as she leaned toward Deborah.

"I guessed that."

"I see what's going on here. Agatha, this was not a good idea, not a good idea at all." William scratched the back of his neck.

"William, I had no idea that you were going to be here. Did you do this deliberately, Aunt Agatha?" Deborah wondered whether Aunt Agatha invited him as well and then forgot about it, but if that were the case, where were the girls and Elizabeth?

"*Jah*, I wanted you both to be here. I want to get to the bottom of things with you two."

Deborah shook her head. "About what?"

"Let's talk about this over dinner, shall we?" Aunt Agatha grinned as though nothing was wrong.

"I can see Deborah feels just as uncomfortable as I feel about this, Aunt Agatha."

"We're two adults and can sort out our own problems," said Deborah. "There's nothing left for us to speak about."

"There is and we can sort it out over dinner," Agatha asked.

"I'm sorry to do this to you after you've gone to the trouble of cooking a meal and everything, but I can't stay." Deborah walked past William to her buggy. It was the second-worst embarrassment in her life. The first was when Agatha had them over for dinner previously.

She couldn't believe Aunt Agatha would deliberately put her in a position like that. It was totally unexpected especially coming from the bishop's aunt. Maybe she wasn't wise like everyone thought.

In her rear-view mirror, she saw William had taken a step back and was talking to Aunt Agatha as though he too was upset.

CHAPTER 26

WHILE DEBORAH WAS DRIVING HOME, she felt bad for walking out when Agatha had gone to so much trouble over dinner, but under the circumstances, she was sure it had been warranted. She'd stop by after school tomorrow and give her apologies. Just as she had laid her hand on the door handle of her *haus,* she heard a buggy and turned to see William. Now she felt doubly bad. He hadn't stayed for Agatha's dinner either. Was he as angry with her as she was with him?

When the horse came to a halt, she walked over to him. "I see you didn't stay either. Are you here to tell me how rude I was just now? Because if you are—"

He jumped out of his buggy. "I'm not mad at you at all. She's a well-meaning person, but I can see how and why you were so upset. It took me by surprise as well. You're the last person I expected to see there tonight."

"Where are Ivy and Grace?"

"With Elizabeth."

"They didn't get invited?"

He shrugged his shoulders, and said, "Aunt Agatha said she had something important to discuss with me and she wanted to discuss it during dinner." He shook his head. "It didn't sound right, but I never expected to see you there. What was she trying to do?"

Deborah relaxed immediately. This time they were on the same side because they were both upset with another person, thus giving them common ground.

"The only thing she could've been doing was trying to get the two of us together." He chuckled, and she suddenly saw the funny side and laughed too.

Then, Deborah rubbed her eyes. "I don't know what I'm going to do now. I didn't prepare anything for dinner." As soon as she said it she regretted it. It sounded like she was throwing out a hint.

"I'm not expected home for some time. Would you like to come out with me for dinner somewhere?"

"Oh no, I couldn't."

"You still haven't forgiven me?"

"It's not that, and besides … have you forgiven me?"

"Why don't we agree to forgive each other? I've missed our conversations."

Slowly, she nodded before she remembered she'd already forgiven him. "Alright. We'll forgive each other." She held out her hand and he shook it, but then he held onto her hand a little bit too long before he released it.

"Now, what are we going to do about food?" he asked. "I'm starving."

"I don't really like going out to eat amongst the *Englischers*."

"Well then, how about I bring us back some takeout?"

She opened her mouth trying to figure out what she wanted. "Okay."

"What do you fancy?"

"I really don't know. Anything will be fine."

"Okay. I'll be back as quick as I can, or would you like to accompany me?"

She thought about her house that she hadn't finished cleaning. If she stayed home, she could make it look really nice by the time he got back. That would make a good impression on him now that they were friends again. "I might stay here if that's all right with you."

"As long as you let me in when I get back."

She giggled. "If you've got food with you I will."

He gave her a big smile, turned, and then hurried to his waiting buggy. As soon as he was gone, she closed the front door and proceeded with the cleaning she had started before she left for Aunt Agatha's. She thought about changing into a more flattering dress, but figured if William was serious about her it wouldn't matter. And if he wasn't, a dress was hardly the answer. Things had moved to a different level with William, she could feel it. There was definitely an attraction between the two of them.

By the time she heard his buggy returning, she'd managed to finish the cleaning and get the fire going.

He was cradling two pizza boxes in one arm and his other hand held onto a white paper bag. "I hope you like pizza with the works."

"I do. I like any kind of pizza."

He lifted up the white bag. "Strawberry and vanilla ice cream for dessert."

"Oooh. I love ice cream. You can come for dinner any time," she said, as he walked in the front door.

He walked past her and then turned back. "Where am I going?"

"Straight ahead and through to the kitchen. I forgot you haven't been here before."

"That's because you never asked me," he said with a cheeky little smile as he placed the pizza boxes down on the table.

She pulled out plates from the cupboard. "They smell delicious."

"I hope so. We'll soon find out. I've had pizza from there before and it's always been good. It's a favorite of the girls'." Then, he passed her the ice cream cartons and she tucked them into the gas-powered freezer.

They prayed first, and then sat in silence while he opened the first box and pushed it toward her. She pulled off a slice and bit into it. There was a quiet moment as they each enjoyed their first mouthful of food.

"This is good. *Denke,* for this."

"You're very welcome. This is the first time we've had a meal together. Just us, I mean."

She nodded, as she'd just taken another bite of pizza. Once she had swallowed, she said, "I do feel badly for Agatha." She started to giggle, tried to stop but met William's eyes and he laughed too. That was it. They both laughed until they were wiping tears from their eyes.

"So do I," he said once they'd finally stopped laughing, "but she took me by surprise."

"Both of us are in the same boat. Tell me this, William. You were so upset with me when you worked out that I was trying to make you jealous with Andrew. Why did you decide to forgive me?"

He placed his slice of pizza down onto his plate. "I thought about what I was losing by being upset with you. I don't know why I was determined in going down that road. Then I realized that I might have done the same thing if I had been in your shoes. You're the woman I want, Deborah, but I never thought you'd look at me so I never gave you a clue I was interested. I'm older and—"

"I know you once invited May to your *haus.* She's so much younger than I am."

He shook his head. "I asked her to come for dinner because I was going to ask her if she'd do a few hours of *haus* cleaning for me on Saturday mornings."

"Oh."

He laughed. "You couldn't have thought I saw myself with May? She's only a little older than my own daughters."

She didn't see the funny side. "I did think that. You'd hardly have been the first man to marry a younger woman."

"Marry me, Deborah?"

She studied his face and there was no hint of a smile. "Are you joking?"

"Nee, I've never been more serious about anything in my life. I don't want there to be any more misunderstand-

173

ings between us. I'm not the judgmental person you think I am." He shrugged. "Maybe I am, but you can make me see sense. See? You suit me."

She giggled. After she'd given up and let go of her heart's desire, he'd come to her. "I don't know what to say. This is all—"

"Say yes to me, Deborah, please? And I will make you happy. That is, if you think you can put up with me and the girls."

Deborah nodded as tears stung behind her eyes. *"Jah,* I will marry you."

He laughed, and she saw tears well in his eyes.

"The only thing is …"

"What?"

She swallowed against the lump in her throat. "You've been married before and I hope you won't compare me. I might not measure up."

"I won't. You're both completely different. And you can make over our house to suit you. I know I left Nita's sewing room just how she had it, but she's gone and I want you to make the place yours. Or, we can move to a different *haus.* Anything that makes you happy."

"Really?"

"Of course. If you're happy then I'll be happy. I am the most blessed man in the world at this moment. I thought you were so far away from me. So unattainable, and now you've agreed to marry me. Are you sure, Deborah?"

"I'm surer than I've been about anything."

"Good. How about we plan our life together over some of that ice cream?"

She giggled. "Okay. We can sit in front of the fire so we don't get too cold."

IN FRONT of a toasty fire in Deborah's living room, she and William planned their wedding and then they discussed plans to reinvent his house to better suit his two growing girls and Deborah. Then they laughed about how surprised Aunt Agatha would be when they told her. And they decided that she'd be the very first person they'd tell.

I hope you enjoyed *The Amish School Teacher*.
Samantha Price

The next book in the series is book 7:
Amish Baby Blessing.

When a young single Amish woman moves to Pleasant Valley and learns of Mervin Breuer, she is determined to 'help' him. It was reported he lived with his grandmother and rarely left home. No one knew whether he was shy or whether he was content to remain a single man forever.

What will she do when she discovers the secret he is keeping from the Amish community?

Mervin doesn't know what he's done to deserve the

attention of this woman, but it's too much. He likes a quiet life and she will not stop talking and not only that, she grates on his last nerve.

How will a stranger's baby cause them to overlook their differences and bring the unlikely pair together?

EXPECTANT AMISH WIDOWS series.

Book 1 Amish Widow's Hope

Book 2 The Pregnant Amish Widow

Book 3 Amish Widow's Faith

Book 4 Their Son's Amish Baby

Book 5 Amish Widow's Proposal

Book 6 The Pregnant Amish Nanny

Book 7 A Pregnant Widow's Amish Vacation

Book 8 The Amish Firefighter's Widow

Book 9 Amish Widow's Secret

Book 10 The Middle-Aged Amish Widow

Book 11 Amish Widow's Escape

Book 12 Amish Widow's Christmas

Book 13 Amish Widow's New Hope

Book 14 Amish Widow's Story

Book 15 Amish Widow's Decision

Book 16 Amish Widow's Trust

Book 17 The Amish Potato Farmer's Widow

AMISH LOVE BLOOMS

Book 1 Amish Rose

Book 2 Amish Tulip

Book 3 Amish Daisy

Book 4 Amish Lily

Book 5 Amish Violet

Book 6 Amish Willow

AMISH BRIDES

Book 1 Arranged Marriage

Book 2 Falling in Love

Book 3 Finding Love

Book 4 Amish Second Loves

Book 5 Amish Silence

AMISH TWIN HEARTS

Book 1 Amish Trading Places

Book 2 Amish Truth Be Told

Book 3 The Big Beautiful Amish Woman

Book 4 The Amish Widow and the Millionaire

AMISH ROMANCE SECRETS

Book 1 A Simple Choice

Book 2 Annie's Faith

Book 3 A Small Secret

Book 4 Ephraim's Chance

Book 5 A Second Chance

Book 6 Choosing Amish

AMISH WEDDING SEASON

Book 1 Impossible Love

Book 2 Love at First

Book 3 Faith's Love

Book 4 The Trials of Mrs. Fisher

Book 5 A Simple Change

For a full list of all Samantha Price's books go to:

www.samanthapriceauthor.com

ABOUT THE AUTHOR

A prolific author of Amish fiction, Samantha Price wrote stories from a young age, but it wasn't until later in life that she took up writing full time. Formally an artist, she exchanged her paintbrush for the computer and, many best-selling book series later, has never looked back.

Samantha is happiest on her computer lost in the world of her characters.

To date, Samantha has received several All Stars Awards; Harlequin has published her Amish Love Blooms series, and Amazon Studios have produced several of her books in audio.

Samantha is best known for the Ettie Smith Amish Mysteries series and the Expectant Amish Widows series.

To learn more about Samantha Price and her books visit:

www.samanthapriceauthor.com

Samantha Price loves to hear from her readers.
samanthaprice333@gmail.com
www.facebook.com/SamanthaPriceAuthor

Follow Samantha Price on BookBub

Twitter @ AmishRomance

Made in the USA
Monee, IL
10 February 2023